James Cook

James Cook

Yahya Ashraf

PARTRIDGE

To order additional copies of this book, contact
Partridge India
000 800 10062 62
orders.india@partridgepublishing.com

www.partridgepublishing.com/india

FOR MY PARENTS & WHO
SUPPORTED ME TO
WRITE THIS BOOK. WITHOUT THEM
THIS BOOK WOULD NEVER EXIST.

HE WAS BORN IN A TOWN OF AMERICA. HIS NAME WAS JAMES HENRY ALBUS COOK. HE HAD NOTHING TO EAT. HIS BRAIN WAS VERY BRILLIANT. BUT WHO KNEW IT. PEOPLE THOUGHT THAT A BEGGAR CAN'T DO ANYTHING. THEY WERE PROBABLY WRONG.

IT WAS DARK WINTER. A MAN WITH BLUE EYES, WHITE FACE, AND LONG HEIGHT, THIN AND LOOKING VERY THIRSTY AND STARVING, WAS BEGGING ON THE ROAD OF AMERICA. THE WEATHER WAS VERY BAD. IT WAS RAINING AND COLD

WINDS WERE BLOWING. THERE WAS SNOW EVERYWHERE.

NO ONE WAS THERE TO HELP HIM, HE WAS VERY POOR. EVERYONE WAS ENJOYING WITH THEIR FAMILY AS IT WAS CHRISTMAS. HE PUT A GOBLET FRONT OF HIM AND HE WAS SITTING ON THE ROAD. ABAFT OF HIM WAS A DENSE FOREST.

HE HEARD A SOUND WHICH SAID THAT COME HERE.

HE WAS VERY SCARED BUT HE WAS BRAVER. HE WENT AND WENT INSIDE THE FOREST. OVER THERE HE SAW BLUE BALL RISING IN THE SKY. IT WAS FLYING. NOT MUCH BUT YES, IT WAS FLYING.

AS HE TOUCHED IT, HE STARTED ROLLING, HE WAS ALSO FLYING BUT IN PAIN, HE WAS RUBBING HIMSELF IN THE GROUND, AFTER A MINUTE HE LAY ON THE GROUND, HE WAS NOT DEAD BUT HE WAS NOT ALIVE. HE FELT UNCONSCIOUS. THE NEXT DAY HE FOUND HIMSELF IN AN UNKNOWN PLACE.. HE DIDN'T REMEMBER ANYTHING. HE ALSO DIDN'T REMEMBER THAT HE WAS POOR.

HE WOKE UP AND WENT IN THE OTHER ROOM. HE WAS IN A BIG PLACE WHICH WAS OF A SCIENTIST BECAUSE THERE WERE CHEMICAL LABS, INVENTION LAB AND MANY OTHER. BUT THERE WAS NO ONE. HE KNEW THAT THIS HOUSE IS OF HIM AND HE IS A SCIENTIST. PEOPLE WERE SHOCKED TO SEE HIM. WHENEVER HE USE TO GO OUT, PEOPLE USE TO ASK HIM THAT WHEN HE CAME IN THIS HOUSE.

JAMES USE TO SNAP PEOPLE AND SAY THAT IT WAS HIS HOUSE. HE FOUND EVERY CHEMICAL AND MECHANICAL THING IN HIS HOUSE.

3 YEARS HAVE PASSED. ON 12 AUGUST 2020 HE WAS SITTING. BEFORE 2 YEARS HE HAD GOT AN IDEA FOR MAKING A THING WHICH COULD DO ANY BIG THING AS SMALL AS AN ANT. HE HAS KEPT THE NAME COMPRESSOR.

AFTER 5 YEARS HE MADE IT. IT WAS A SMALL TIN BOX. THERE WERE TWO ROUND THINGS WHICH WERE CALLED DIGREEAR. IT WAS USED TO SET THAT HOW MUCH SMALL YOU HAVE TO DO THE THING. THERE WAS A RED BUTTON.

WHEN YOU PRESS THE BUTTON, THE COMPRESSOR ON. YOU HAVE TO PUT ON THE BIG THING WHICH YOU HAVE TO DO SMALL. THE COMPRESSOR SCANS THE THING AND IT BECOMES SMALL. BUYING A COMPRESSOR IS A FORTUNE. BECAUSE OF THIS INVENTION, HE BECAME VERY FAMOUS.

AFTER THIS INVENTION HE MADE MANY MORE THINGS. SOON HE BECAME FAMOUS VERY FAMOUS. HE WAS THE FOURTH RICHEST MAN OF THE WORLD. HE WROTE MANY BOOKS TOO WHICH BROUGHT MORE FAME TOWARDS HIM. HE WAS FOND OF GOING TO ANOTHER PLACE. ONE DAY HE WENT TO INDIA AND HE SAW THAT A PERSON WAS DEAD. OVER THERE IN HIS MIND HE GOT AN IDEA FOR MAKING ELIXIR. AFTER TWO THREE DAYS HE DEVICE THE PLAN AND ORDERED 100 MUMMIES FROM EGYPT TO MAKE THEM ALIVE.

IN THE WHOLE WORLD THIS NEWS WAS KNOWN BY EVERYONE. THOUSANDS OF PEOPLE AND SOME MORE WITH A PAPER ON WHICH WAS WRITTEN 'JAMES IS GREAT' WENT TOWARDS HIS HOUSE

HOWLING. THEY REACHED AT HIS HOUSE. AT THAT TIME ONLY HE WOKE UP AND WAS DRINKING COFFEE. HE HEARD THE SOUND OF PEOPLE SHOUTING 'JAMES IS GREAT.' HE WENT OUT AND WEAVED HIS HAND. AFTER AN HOUR HE WENT INSIDE. HE PICKED UP THE NEWS PAPER WHICH WAS LYING ON THE FLOOR. THE HEADLINES WERE 'JAMES COOK THE NEXT EINSTEIN AND DOWN WAS WRITTEN 'THE CHOSEN ONE.' IN HIS LAB THERE IS A SECRET ROOM. HE HAD KEPT OVER THERE THE FORMULAE OF MAKING ELIXIR. AND FROM HERE THE STORY BEGINS.

ONE DAY HE WAS SITTING ON THE BED OF THE LAB AND THINKING FOR HIS ELIXIR, HE GOT A PHONE CALL. HE PICKED IT UP. THE CALLER SAID "IS JAMES COOK SPEAKING?' HE SAID, 'YES I AM ONLY SPEAKING AND WHO ARE YOU? THE CALLER SAID, 'I WOULD START WITH MY INTRODUCTION LATER BUT I THE OWNER OF EGYPT IS SPEAKING, I HAD CALLED YOU TO ASK THAT YOU ARE ONLY THE PERSON WHO HAS ORDERED 150 MUMMIES? JAMES SAID, 'YES'.

YOUR COST IS $100000 AND IF IT WOULD SUPPLY BY THE SHIP THEN IT WOULD TAKE $1000 EXTRA. JAMES SAID, 'OK I WOULD COME IN EGYPT TOMORROW AND I HAVE LESS MONEY SO YOU GIVE HIM THEN 100 MUMMIES.' THE CALLER SAID THAT OK, AND THEN YOUR PRICE WOULD BE $50000.'

JAMES SAID, 'GIVE ME THEN IN $40000.' HE SAID THAT OK I WOULD COME TOMORROW TO EGYPT. AS HE PUT THE CALL HE WENT STRAIGHT TO THE BANK AND TOOK OUT 60000$. 40000$ FOR THE MUMMIES 10000$ FOR THE PETROL OF HIS CHARTED PLANE AND 10000 FOR THE HOTEL IN EGYPT. HE PACKED HIS BAG WITH HIS EVERYTHING OF HIS LAB. HE TOOK HIS COMPRESSER AND THE GIFTS FOR HIS RELATIVES WHO LIVED IN EGYPT. HE ALSO TOOK HIS ANYTHING DETECTOR WHICH CAN TELL US WHAT IS INSIDE OF ANYTHING.

IN THE MORNING HE TOOK HIS LAB AND IT IS POSSIBLE WITH THE COMPRESSOR. THE COMPRESSOR'S RETAIL VALUE WAS $100,000,000 THING WHICH HE HAS TO

TAKE FOR HIS JOURNEY. HE SAT IN HIS CHARTED PLANE. HE KNEW HOW TO DRIVE IT SO HE DIDN'T NEED ANY DRIVER. WHEN HE WAS IN THE MIDDLE OF HIS JOURNEY HE THOUGHT TO CHECK IN HIS GIFTS WHICH HE HAS BROUGHT FOR HIS RELATIVES. THERE WAS A SYSTEM FROM WHICH THE PLANE CAN FLY ON ITS OWN.

HE PRESSED THE BUTTON AND WENT TO SEE THE GIFTS. HE DID NOT KNOW WHAT IS INSIDE IT BECAUSE HIS SERVANT CHRISTINO DAVID HAD FORGOT TO TELL HIM WHAT IS INSIDE IT AND HE DID NOT KNOW HOW TO TIE THE GIFT RAPPER BACK.

MR. DAVID WAS NEVER A GOOD SERVANT. ONE DAY THAT MAN BROKE HENRY'S FAVORITE VASE. SO HE BEAT HIM A LOT AND THEN IT ALWAYS SEEMED THAT HE WANTED KILL HIM.

ONE FINE DAY WHEN HE WAS GOING TO HIS LAB, ON THE STAIR CASE HE FOUND OIL. NEXT TIME DAVID TRIED TO PUT THE POISON IN HIS FOOD BUT IT WAS HIS BAD LUCK THAT HE PUT THE ROSE JUICE INSTEAD OF POISON AND IT TASTED WELL.

THIS ALL JAMES DIDN'T KNOW BUT ONE DAY BY MISTAKE HE GAVE HIM HIS PHONE AND WHEN HE WAS MIXING THE POISON HE CLICKED SELFIES AND HE FORGOT TO DO IT OFF AND A VIDEO WAS MADE. JAMES NEVER WANTED TO TAKE HIM OUT BECAUSE HE WAS VERY POOR BUT HE THOUGHT THAT HE WOULD GIVE HIM THE LAST WARNING. SURELY JAMES WAS OF BIG HEART.

THINKING THIS ONLY HE TOOK OUT HIS ANYTHING DETECTOR AND WHEN TO SEE THE GIFTS. THE FIRST WAS A VASE, SECOND ONE WAS A LAPTOP, THIRD ONE WAS RC HELICOPTER, FOURTH ONE SAID BOMB HE THOUGHT WHAT IS INSIDE IT SO HE OPENED IT AND SAW A BOMB, JAMES TOOK HIS PARASUIT AND HE JUMPED FROM THE PLANE.

FLAMES WERE COMING OUT FROM THE PLANE. THE BACK WING WAS FIRED AND THEN THE OTHER ALSO. JAMES KNEW THAT HE WOULD DIE SO HE TOOK OUT A SMALL AIRBOAT FROM HIS COMPRESSOR. THE LANDING WAS FINE. BUT IT WAS ON WATER. MID OF WATER.

IT WAS ACTUALLY SEA.

HE KNEW THAT HE WOULD SINK FAST AND HE WOULD DIE IN ONE OR TWO MIN. SO HE QUICKLY TOOK OUT HIS SINKER. IT WAS A GADGET WHICH CAN HELP YOU NOT TO SINK. HE PUT THE SINKER IN THE AIRBOAT.

JAMES SAT ON IT TO REACH THE SHORE BUT JUST HE STARTED HIS JOURNEY ITS AIR CAME OUT. AS IT CAME OUT, JAMES APPLIED A SALOTAPE ON IT SO THAT MORE AIR DOESN'T COME OUT. AND THEN HE SLEPT ON IT. HE SLEPT FOR ONE HOUR. HE WAS ACTUALLY NOT ABLE TO SLEEP.

HE WAS LOOKING AT THE CLOUDS AT THAT TIME ONLY WAVES STARTED COMING.

A GIGANTIC WAVE THREW JAMES ON AN UNKNOWN PLACE. IT WAS A CRUISE LINER. HE JUST SNUGGLED HIMSELF SOMEWHERE IN A CORNER SO THAT HE IS OUT OF THE SIGH OF ANY ONE. IT WAS NOT TOO LONG WHEN A MAN SAW HIM. A MAN WITH LONG FACE, LONG BEARD, BIG HEIGHT AND PEAKY FACE CAME TOWARDS HENRY. HE SAID WHO THE HELL YOU ARE? JAMES STARTED CHANTING GOD'S NAME. OH! OH! MY GOODNESS YOU ARE HNERY ALBUS. I NEED YOUR AUTOGRAPH, SIR. BUT I SUPPOSE THAT YOU SHOULD BE NOT HERE. 'YES YES, 'SAID HENRY. WOULD YOU HELP ME? WHICH HELP? JAMES THEN TOLD HIM THE WHOLE STORY.

SO, WHERE YOU HAVE TO GO? EGYPT. OK, LET ME SEE THE MAP. 'WE ARE JUST NOW IN RED SEA AND WE HAVE CROSSED SUDAN AND THE NEXT DESTINATION IS EGYPT! 'SAID THAT MAN, LOOKING IN THE MAP. SO YOU WOULD BE AT YOUR DESTINATION. GOODNIGHT. M.R. SCIENTIST.

HE PULLED A WORKER TOWARDS HNERY AND SAID HIM TO SHOW ME MY ROOM. JAMES WAS ON CLOUD NINE!

IT WAS AN AC ROOM WITH A SWIMMING POOL. TWO BROWN CURTAINS WERE HANGING ON THE WINDOW SIDE BUT IT HAD NO EFFECT BECAUSE IT WAS VERY THING. THERE WAS A HUGE BED OF PINK COLOR.

THERE WAS A WASHROOM AT THE CORNER OF THE ROOM. JAMES WAS VERY HAPPY. HE TOOK A PLUNGE IN THE WATER AND DECIDED TO GO AROUND THE SHIP. BUT FIRST HE SLEPT A BIT. AFTER 3 HOURS OF SLEEP, HE WOKE UP. HE TOOK OUT HIS FAVORITE BOOK 'BLACK BEAUTY' AND STARTED READING IT. AFTER AN HOUR HE WENT ABAFT OF THE SHIP. IT WAS NOT A HUGE CRUISE LINER BUT IT WAS A SMALL ONE.

THERE WERE NOT MANY HIGH – END MALLS BUT THEY WERE SMALL. THERE WAS ONE GYM, 4 CINEMA HALL, 1 BOOK HALL (A PLACE TO READ BOOKS) THERE WERE MANY RESTAURANTS WHICH SERVED THE BEST QUSINS OF THE WORLD.

AT THE ABAFT, PEOPLE WERE MAKING FOOD. THERE WERE TOTAL 800 PEOPLE ON THE SHIP.

CHILDREN WERE PLAYING, HOPPING AND SLEEPING. THERE WERE MANY RIDES TO ENJOY. MANY PEOPLE WERE IN THE SWIMMING POOL. SOME OLD PEOPLE WERE DOING YOGA IN YOGA HALL. SOME WERE READING BOOKS. EVERYONE WAS ENJOYING. EVERYONE HAS NOTICED HIM AND WAS TAKING HIS AUTOGRAPH.

WHEN HE WAS FREE, HE WENT TO THE ROOM. BUT HE WAS LOST. JAMES HAS FIRST ALSO BEEN IN CRUISE LINER BUT THIS ONE WAS NICER.

JAMES WAS ROAMING AROUND IT LIKE AN INUIT. JAMES FELT VERY EMBARRASSED. BECAUSE HE HAS NOT GAVE THEM THE MONEY AND HE WAS ON THE SHIP WITHOUT GIVING ANY FEES. SO HE DECIDED TO GIVE THEM HIS 10000$. HE WAS LOST BUT HE TOOK A HELP OF A WORKER AND HE REACHED.

HE QUICKLY TOOK OUT HIS MONEY AND HE WENT TOWARDS THE OFFICE. IT WAS LIKE A MAZE. IT TOOK HALF AN HOUR TO

FIND THE OFFICE. AT LAST HE FOUND IT.
HE WENT TO THE CAPTAIN AND STARTED
TALKING. SIR, THIS IS THE FEES. NO, JAMES
DOESN'T PAY IT. JAMES KEPT THE MONEY
ON THE WOODEN TABLE AND RAN AWAY.
AFTER GIVING THE MONEY, HE WENT TO
HIS ROOM AND HE STARTED THINKING OF
THE PEOPLE LOVE TOWARDS HIM.

WHEN HE WAS SITTING IN HIS ROOM HE
GOT A CALL.

HE PICKED THE CALL AND IT SAID THAT
I THE OWNER OF EGYPT'S MUSEUM WANT
TO ASK THAT YOU ARE ONLY THE PERSON
WHO HAS ORDERED 100 MUMMIES? HE
SAID, 'YES.' THE MAN SAID THAT HE IS
FEELING VERY SORROW TO TELL HIM
THAT HE CAN GET THE MUMMIES ONLY IN
ONE CONDITION. JAMES SAID THAT WHICH
CONDITION?

THE CALLER SAID THE CONDITION
IS THAT WE HAD ALSO GOT ONE MORE
ORDER FOR 100 MUMMIES BUT WE ARE
HAVING JUST 101 MUMMIES. AND NOW WE
CAN GIVE ONLY 100 TO 1 AND 1 TO 1.

DO YOU WANT 100 MUMMIES ONLY? HE
SAID 'YES I WANT HUNDRED MUMMIES

AND YOU KNOW THAT WHY I WANT IT, IT'S IMPORTANT...' OK FOR THIS CONFUSION ONLY WE HAD MADE A DECISION THAT YOU BOTH WOULD COME TO AN AUCTION HALL AND OVER THERE WHO WOULD PUT THE MOST BIG BID HE WOULD GET IT.

THAT WE HAD TO COME WHERE? YOU HAVE TO COME NEAR RULK AND GULK BAKERY.

CAN WE BRING SOME THINGS WHICH ARE VALUABLE?

THIS JAMES SAID BECAUSE HE WAS HAVING A LITTLE MONEY. JAMES ASKED, 'CAN YOU TELL ME THAT WHERE THE BID CAN GO? 'THE BID CAN GO ABOVE 100000 ALSO.' SAID THE CALLER. WHEN HE SAID THIS WORD, JAMES FELT VERY BAD BECAUSE HE WAS JUST HAVING 60000 IN HIS POCKET. THE CALLER SAID THAT YES YOU CAN BRING SOME VALUABLE THINGS BUT REALLY VALUABLE.

JAMES TOOK A SIGH OF RELIEF AND SAID THAT THEN THERE IS NO PROBLEM I WOULD BRING 11000000 IN MY POCKET. I GUESS YOU ARE NOT BRINGING CHECK.

NO I AM NOT BRINGING A CHECK BUT A COMPRESSOR. THE CALLER DIDN'T UNDERSTAND ANYTHING. WHICH TYPE OF COMPRESSOR AND WHAT IS A COMPRESSOR? HNERY DIDN'T WANT TO TELL HIM THE WHOLE THING ABOUT IT SO HE SAID THAT NO IT'S NOTHING. HE SAID "BUT YOU COME OR YOU WOULD LOSE YOUR 100 MUMMIES.'

WHEN WE HAVE TO COME AND AT WHICH TIME? SIR WE WOULD MASSAGE YOU THE WHOLE ADDRESS AND AT WHICH TIME AND WHEN, OK. HNERY KEPT THE CALL AND HE WENT FOR SWIMMING. AFTER SOMETIME JAMES GOT A MESSAGE WHICH SAID

GOOD MORNING M.R ALBUS. AS WE HAVE FIRST ONLY GIVEN YOU THE HALF IN FORMATION AND WE HAVE TO GIVE YOU NOW THE MAIN INFORMATION

ADDRESS – NEAR RULK AND HULK BAKERY, IT IS BESIDE CHURCH STREET.

NAME OF THE AUCTION HALL- FIST BIG HALL

NAME OF THE PERSON – LAPASCO KNITTER AND HE IS IN A BIG UNIVERSITY AND HE IS THE PRINCIPAL OF IT.

M.R. ALBUS PLEASE COME

AFTER SOMETIME HE WENT TO SLEEP. BUT I WAS NOT ABLE TO SLEEP SO I THOUGHT TO GO TO THE MANAGER AND ASK HIM THAT WHY THERE IS NO SUNLIGHT AND WE ARE IN THE MIDDLE HOW IT CAN BE THAT WE ARE IN SEA AND THERE IS NO SUNLIGHT NOR DARK IT WAS A PLEASANT DAY BUT HOW IT CAN BE?

JAMES WAS THINKING A LOT ABOUT IT SO HE WENT ON HIS WAY TOWARDS THE MANAGER. WHEN HE STARTED TO GO HE HEARD A NOISE. IT SAID THAT GOOD MORNING EVERY ONE, I AM FEELING VERY BAD TO TELL YOU THAT WE ARE VERY SORRY TO MAKE YOUR GOOD MORNING A BAD MORNING.

THIS CAN BE YOUR LAST BREATHE. WHEN HE SAID THEASE WORDS, MOST OF THE PEOPLE WERE THINKING WHAT IT IS AND WHEN THE SECOND NEWS CAME, THOSE PEOPLE SAID WHAT THE HELL THIS IS. THE BAD NEWS WAS THAT A TERRIBLE HURRICANE IS COMING TOWARDS US IN ONE HOUR.

JAMES LOOKED UP. THE SKY WAS BLUE AND COLD WINDS WERE BLOWING, THIS MEANS THAT THEY WILL LEAVE THEM IN A PLACE AND GO AWAY FROM THERE SO THAT THEY GET MORE PROFIT. HE WENT TO THE CAPTAIN OFFICE. THE CAPTAIN WAS SITTING ON A CHAIR AND WAS TALKING WITH HIMSELF.

HE WAS MURMURING THAT IS WHY HE DIDN'T HEAR HIM. HE WAS NOT THE CAPTAIN BUT THE MANAGER. IT WAS A BIG ROOM WITH A WIND AND A CHAIR. THERE WAS AN AC AND A TV

HE WAS DRINKING COLD PUMPKIN JUICE. JAMES SAID, 'YOU BLOODY FRAUDS. 'THE MANAGER SAID, 'WHAT ARE YOU SAYING M.R ALBUS.

I KNOW WHAT I AM SAYING!

MIND YOUR LANGUAGE.

YOU MIND YOUR LANGUAGE. DON'T YOU FEEL ASHAMED OF DOING THIS? WHAT ARE YOU SAYING?

SHUT UP MR. ROLED. WHAT ARE YOU TALKING, JUST SAY STRAIGHTLY. OH! TRYING TO BE VERY SMART.

I WON'T CARE NOW THAT YOU ARE JAMES COOK, I WOULD JUST THROW YOU FROM THE SHIP. YOU CAN'T DO THIS. I HAVE PAYED $10000 FOR THE SHIP AND FOR ONLY ONE DAY.

YOU DON'T REMEMBER OR I MAKE YOU. JAMES WAS VERY ANGRY. HE SAID THAT IF I WANT THEN I CAN SEND YOU TO PRISON AND OVER THERE YOU MAKE PEOPLE FOOL.

I WOULD TELL YOU WHAT YOU HAD DONE. IT LOOKS VERY STRANGE THAT THE CLOUDS ARE BLUE AND HOW A TERRIBLE HURRICANE IS COMING AND HOW YOU KNOW THE EXACT TIME WITHOUT ANY RADIO OR TV? HOW YOU KNOW TELL ME! YOU CAN MAKE OTHERS FOOL BUT NOT ME.

JAMES COOK THE CHOSEN ONE. HNERY YOU ARE SO FAMOUS AND INTELLIGENT. I FIRST ALSO KNEW THAT YOU ARE VERY INTELLIGENT BUT TODAY I AM SEEING IT.

YOU ARE WRONG. BUT IF YOU WANT THEN SEE. THEN JAMES NOTICED THAT A WOODEN STICK WAS LYING BEHIND HIM. ROLED TOOK THE STICK AND SAID 'RIO TRISM HURRICUN.'

AFTER THIS THERE ONLY A MAN CAME AND HE SAT DOWN. IN A MATTER OF SECONDS THE HURRICANE WAS ABLE TO SEE. HOW YOU DID IT? MAGIC. THERE IS NOTHING LIKE MAGIC. THERE IS.

YOU WILL GET TO KNOW AFTER 3 DAYS.

WHEN YOU WILL BE KILLED. WHO WILL KILL ME? JAMES LOOKED A LITTLE PUZZLED AND FEAR WAS EASILY SEEN IN HIS EYES. SATEN. WHO IS HE? MASTER OF MAGIC. NO ONE IS LIKE HIM. BUT ONE PERSON CAN BECOME LIKE HIM BY MARVELLE (SAY MAR – VELLE LOCKET.

WHAT IS THIS NOW? BOOK. DON'T TALK RUBBISH.

HOW A BOOKS NAME IS MARVELLE LOCKET. IF SOMEONE WANTS IT SO IT SHOULD BE FAMOUS AND I HAVE HEARD NO BOOK'S NAME LIKE THIS. YOU HAVE FORGOT. WHO HAVE THIS BOOK?

YOUR PARENTS. I DON'T HAVE ANY PARENTS. YOU HAVE. YOU ARE MAD. THERE TALKS WERE ABSTRUSE TO HIM.

JAMES PICKED UP HIS CALLER AND SAID HIM TO TELL HIM THE THINGS CLEARLY.

HE PICKED UP THE GUN WHICH WAS ON THE DESK AND THE RELOADED IT. AND HE AS HE WAS GOING TO SHOOT HIM, THE MAN WHO WAS THERE STOOD UP AND THEN SAID 'REPITCULOUS.'(SAY REPI – CULOUS) THANKS.

SO HOW TO BE SAVED BY THIS CONDITION. THE MAN SAID 'I AM GOING TO DO A BROKEL FROM WHICH HE WILL THINK THAT EVERYTHING IS FINE AND THEN HE WILL RETURN TO HIS ROOM AND BRING A THING FROM WHICH WE CAN STOP THE HURRICUN AND LORD SATEN WOULD BE ALSO HAPPY FROM US.

OK DO FAST. THE MAN PICKED UP THE STICK AND SAID 'STRAYED 'AFTER SOMETIME JAMES WOKE UP AND HE WENT TOWARDS HIS ROOM. HE DIDN'T REMEMBER THAT WHAT HAS HAPPENED. HE JUST REMEMBERED THAT THERE IS A GLASS FROM WHICH THEY ARE NOT ABLE TO SEE THE HURRICANE. IT WAS PUT SO THAT THE TOURISTS CAN ENJOY.

JAMES TOOK A GADGET FROM WHICH THE SHIPS CAN FLY AND HE WENT AND

GAVE IT TO THE CAPTAIN. SOON THE SHIP ROSE IN THE AIR AND WENT TOWARDS EGYPT. AFTER AN HOUR JAMES REACHED IN EGYPT.

NEXT DAY JAMES SAT IN A CAR
AND REACHED THE HALL. THEY WERE
SITTING ON THE WOODEN CHAIR. IT WAS
A PRETTY SMALL ROOM WITH A SMALL
STAGE. THE OWNER CAME AND HE SAID
THAT HELLO FRIENDS I THOMAS WOULD
START THE AUCTION IN THE PRESENT
DAY IN 1 MINUTE. THE HUNDRED MUMMIES
WERE KEPT BESIDE HIM.

A MAN WITH NO BEARD OR MOUSTACHE
WAS SITTING VERY FAR.

HE WAS LAPESCO. HE WORE A BLACK
SUIT AND WAS CARRYING LOTS OF MONEY.

THE BIDDING STARTED. LAPASCO SAID - - $1000. THE AUCTIONEER SAID, 'SIR, IT'S LOOKING LIKE YOU HAD COME IN THE MARKET TO BUY VEGETABLES.

JAMES WAS A LITTLE HAPPY BECAUSE THE BIDDING WAS GOING IN CONTROL SO HE ALSO SAID LITTLE ONLY.

HE SAID $1500.

JAMES GOT A SHOCK FROM BACK, LAPASCO SAID - - $50000.

JAMES SAID - $50500.

LAPASCO SAID - - $80000, IT WENT OUT OF HENRY'S BUDGET.

JAMES SAID - $85000.

LAPASCO SAID - - $90000.

JAMES SAID - $90500.

AFTER THAT WE HEARD A VOICE WHICH SHOOK US.

LAPASCO SAID - - $200000.

JAMES THOUGHT THAT HE HAD LOST.

THE AUCTIONEER SAID 1 2 AND AS HE WAS GOING TO SAY 3, JAMES SAID - 205000.

LAPASCO SAID - - 206000.

WHEN LAPASCO SAID - - 206000 THEN JAMES GOT TO KNOW THAT LAPASCO HAD NO LESS MONEY SO HE CAN WIN.

JAMES SAID -270000.

LAPASCO SAID - - 207500 AND THEN JAMES SAID 217000. IT WAS SILENT AND THE AUCTIONEER SAID 1 2 AND 3 AND NOW THE 100 MUMMIES ARE OF M.R ALBUS.

JAMES GAVE THEM HIS LASER GUN AND IT WAS ALSO SIGNED AND HE ALSO GAVE THEM HIS LAPTOP.

HE LEFT THE HALL AND CAME OUT.

HE WAS NOT HAVING ONE PENNY ALSO SO HE DECIDED TO SELL HIS LAB THINGS.

JAMES SOLD SOME THINGS AND HE GOT 30000; HE MADE HIS LAB OVER THERE ONLY BECAUSE HE WAS HAVING A LITTLE MONEY SO HE COULD NOT GO TO AMERICA BECAUSE NEITHER HE WAS HAVING HIS PLANE AND NOR HE WAS HAVING HIS PHONE. HE WENT TO HIS LAB AND HE OPENED HIS SECRET ROOM, IN THAT SECRET ROOM HE WAS HAVING 20G OF HIMSTRATE. IT WAS A POWDER WHICH CAN MAKE OUR BONE MARROW ALIVE.

HE WAS HAVING 20G OF HAERDECHHIMR;
IT WAS A POWDER WHICH CAN MAKE OUR
HEART ALIVE.

HE WAS HAVING 20G OF IMUNITITY, IT
CAN MAKE OUR IMMUNITY SYSTEM ALIVE.
HE WAS HAVING 20G OF KIDNEYER; IT
WAS A POWDER WHICH CAN MAKE OUR
KIDNEY ALIVE. HE WAS HAVING 20G OF
INTERNAL; IT WAS A POWDER WHICH CAN
MAKE OUR EYES, EARS, NOSE, TONGUE,
HAND, LEG, SKIN AND LUNGS ALIVE. HE
WAS HAVING 30G OF BREINOS, IT CAN
MAKE OUR BRAIN ALIVE, HE WAS HAVING
20G OF VACATIONER, AND IT WOULD ACT
LIKE A PROTECTION AGAINST EVERY
DISEASE POSSIBLE.

HE WAS ALSO HAVING 20G OF OTHER;
IT CAN MAKE OTHER ORGANS ALIVE. ALL
THE CHEMICALS LOOKED LIKE ABSINTHE.
HE TOOK A YUNGOSTIC CHEMICAL WHICH
WAS MADE BY HIM AND HE PLACED
IT ON THE TABLE. JAMES TOOK THE
OTHER CHEMICAL AND HE ADDED IT IN
YUNGOSTIC CHEMICAL. JAMES BOILED IT
AND HE ADDED SALT IN IT.

HE TOOK A BEAKER HOLDER AND PUT THE MIXED CHEMICAL IN IT. HE ADDED A BIT OF SUGAR AND THEN ACID. AS HE ADDED THE ACID, FIRE CAME OUT. HE PUT A LITTLE WATER AND AFTER THAT HE WORE HIS GLOVES WHICH WERE A SPECIAL TYPE OF GLOVES. JAMES HAD MADE IT BECAUSE THE CHEMICALS WERE VERY DANGEROUS. HE LEFT THE CHEMICALS STAY IN HEAT AND AFTER 1 HOUR IT TURNED INTO A JELLY. AFTER 1 HOUR IT TURNED IN A SOLID MATTER.

AFTER AN HOUR HE BROUGHT IT BACK. HE MADE VERY SMALL TABLETS OF IT BY BREAKING IT AND AT LAST ELIXIR WAS MADE. HE STARTED PUTTING THE TABLETS IN EVERY MUMMY'S MOUTH. BUT NOTHING HAPPENED. HE WAS VERY SAD.

JAMES WENT TO WASHROOM TO COOL OFF. WHEN HE WAS IN THE WASHROOM HE GOT TO KNOW THAT HE HAD PUT RC POWDER INSTEAD OF WC POWER. RC POWDER IS A POWDER WHICH COULD MAKE A PERSON DO BAD THINGS AND WC POWDER IS JUST ITS OPPOSITE.

HE HAD BROUGHT JUST WC POWDER ONLY THAT IS WHY HE DIDN'T LOOK THE PACKET. RC POWDER WAS MADE BY MISTAKE. WHEN HE WAS DOING RESEARCH ON HIS CHEMICALS AND HE WAS MIXING THEM THEN HE MIXED OTHER CHEMICAL AND THE PATTERN WAS ALSO WRONG SO RC POWDER WAS MADE. HE COULD NOT JUST THROW IT SO HE THOUGHT TO BURN IT BUT WHEN HE WAS GOING TO BURN HE GOT A PHONE CALL SO HE FORGOT COMPLETELY ABOUT IT. JAMES KNEW THAT THE BOMB AND RC POWDER WAS KEPT BY CHRISTINO. JAMES QUICKLY RAN BUT IT WAS LATE. JAMES FELT LIKE THE WORLD HAD BEEN DESTROYED.

THE MUMMIES HAD COME ALIVE.

It was whole green. The smoke was making James cough a lot. The mummies were attacking his lab. One mummy picked him up and threw him. James hid himself under a chair. The mummies made a position like army and started walking. They were looking very shrewish. When the mummies were walking it looked like a seismic. They tried to sedative James with their power. They seethe there selves and started to charge towards the city. James came out of his lab shouting, 'RUN! RUN! RUN! AWAY

MUMMIES HAD COME ALIVE!'IT WAS LIKE A MANTAGE (PART OF A FILM) FROM A FILM MUMMY 1.

FIRST THEY DIDN'T BELIEVE JAMES BUT WHEN THEY SAW THE MUMMIES THEY STARTED RUNNING HERE AND THERE. THEY WENT UNCONSCIOUS.

THEY BROKE MANY BUILDING. IT TOPPLED OVER MANY CARS. JAMES QUICKLY WENT IN HIS LAB AND TOOK HIS COMPRESSOR AND CAME OUT.

HIS LAB WAS DESTROYED BUT HE HAD ALL THE THINGS IN HIS COMPRESSOR. HIS LAB WAS ACTUALLY BURNED BECAUSE SOME HARMFUL CHEMICALS GOT MIXED AND THERE WAS A FIRE AS THE REACTION. THEY WEMT TO PEOPLE 'S HOUSES AND KILLED THEM. THEY GOT RID OF THEIR BANDAGES. THEY WENT TO A MORASS AND KILLED MANY ANIMALS.

JAMES CONCEALED HIMSELF IN A CAVE WHERE HE COULD NOT BE SEEN. HE WAS SEEING ALL THIS THINGS WITH THE HELP OF A CAMERA THAT JAMES PUT ON THE MUMMIES WHEN HE BOUGHT THEM.

THE POLICE CAME TO PUT A KIBOSH ON THEM BUT THEY WERE DEAD.

EVERYONE WAS DEAD IN EGYPT LEAVING HENRY. JAMES CAME OUT OF THE CAVE BUT TO HIS SURPRISE HE SAW THAT THERE WAS A PLANE AND ALL THE MUMMIES WERE STANDING BESIDE IT. THEY SAW HENRY. JAMES FELT LIKE HE WAS GOING TO HELL.

JAMES WAS THINKING THAT THERE SHOULD BE A TIME MACHINE SO THAT HE COULD GO BACK IN TIME. HE HAD ONLY RAISED THE WORLD WITH HIS INVENTIONS BUT NOW BECAUSE OF HIS ONE ABERRATION MISTAKE THE WORLD WILL BE DESTRUCTED.

JAMES THOUGHT THAT HE SHOULD TAKE THEM TO AMERICA. THE MUMMIES MADE JAMES IN THEIR CONTROL. JAMES FLEW THE PLANE AND THEY REACHED AMERICA. THE MUMMIES PUSHED JAMES AND THREW HIM OUT OF THEIR WAY. JAMES SURELY GOT TO KNOW THAT SOMEONE IS CONTROLLING THEM.

JAMES STOOD AND WENT TO HIDE. HE ACTUALLY DIDN'T CONCEAL HIMSELF BUT

HE MADE HIS LAB IN AN AREA WHERE NO ONE WAS THERE. HE WANTED TO MAKE WC POWDER AND HE WOULD SOMEHOW MAKE THEM EAT IT. BUT JAMES WAS WATCHING THE SCENE ALSO. HE QUICKLY TOOK A PAPER AND A PEN. HE STARTED WRITING THE CHEMICALS WHICH HE HAD USED TO MAKE WC POWDER. IT WAS A LIST OF 9 CHEMICALS. BUT IN THAT, TWO WERE THERE WHICH HE WAS NOT HAVING. SO HE HAS TO MAKE THE CHEMICALS WHICH WOULD MAKE THOSE 2 CHEMICALS. SOON HE STARTED HIS WORK. AFTER 5 HOUR 1 CHEMICAL WAS MADE. AFTER MAKING THE CHEMICAL, HE THOUGHT TO NOW LOOK WHAT IS HAPPENING. HE SAW THAT THE MUMMIES WERE KILLING PEOPLE BADLY. PEOPLE WERE STEPPING ON EACH OTHER SOME PEOPLE WERE IN THEIR HOUSE. IT WAS A HELTER-SKELTER.

THE NYPD CAME BUT THEY WERE NOT ABLE TO DO ANYTHING. JAMES WAS VERY SCARED. THE IRATE MUMMIES WERE GOING TO THE REGATTA. SOME MUMMIES WENT TO A LIBRARY.

THEY PUT A FIRE IN THE LIBRARY
AND SOON THE FIRE BROKE OUT IN THE
HOUSE NEAR THE LIBRARY THAN IN
ANOTHER AND ANOTHER. IT WENT TO
A PETROL PUMP AND FROM THERE IT
PUT THE OIL IN EVERY HOUSE AND SOON
HALF OF THE AMERICA WAS ABLAZING
AND AFTER SOMETIME IT GOT BURNED.
PEOPLE CAME OUT OF THEIR HOUSES BUT
THEY WERE SAVED TILL THAT TIME ONLY
WHEN THEY WERE ON THE DOORMAT
BUT AS THEY CAME OUT THERE WERE
MUMMIES EVERYWHERE BECAUSE THEY
HAD REPRODUCED AND THEIR BECAME
TO 1000 AND THE MOST BAD THING WAS
THAT THE ANIMALS WERE WAITING FOR
DINNER AS THEY WERE IN CONTROL OF
THE MUMMIES. THEIR EYES WERE RED
AND THEY WERE NOT FLYING ACTUALLY
BUT THEY WERE RISING INTO THE AIR 10
M HIGH SO THAT THEY CAN'T BE TAKEN
AWAY WITH THE FIRE.

IN 1 HOUR AMERICA WAS DESTROYED
AND $1000000000000 PROPERTY WAS
DESTROYED. JAMES THOUGHT HE WAS A
JINX FOR THE WORLD. JAMES THOUGHT

WHEREAS GOD ERECTS A HOUSE DEVIL BUILDS A CHAPEL THERE, AND WOULD BE FOUND UPON EXAMINATION. OH! GOD PLEASE NO MORE EXAMINATION. THE PRICE OF DARKNESS IS A GENTLEMAN. HOW ART THOU FALLEN FROM HEAVEN, O LUCIFER SON OF THE MORNING.

THIS ALL WERE THE FAMOUS QUOTATION WHICH HE HAD READ AND NOW HE WAS FEELING IT THAT IT WAS REAL. JAMES WAS HIDING IN A SAFE HOUSE WHERE NO BAD PERSON COULD ENTRE AND IF HE TRIES SO HE WOULD GET A CURRENT. THEN WHAT JAMES SAW HE GOT A SHOCK. HE SAW THAT THE MUMMIES WERE COMING TOGETHER AND SOON 100M TALL AND 10M WIDE MUMMIES STARTED DESTROYING EVERYTHING.

THE SOLDIERS OF AMERICA CAME BUT THEY WERE VERY LESS BECAUSE THOUSANDS OF THEM WERE KILLED AND MANY WERE INJURED AND MANY LEFT AMERICA. THE SOLDIERS WERE STANDING IN ONE SIDE WITH THEIR ARMORS AND THE MUMMIES WERE STANDING FRONT OF THEM. THE MUMMIES SPOKE SOMETHING

IN MUMMIES' LANGUAGE AND THEN A COFFIN CAME OUT OF THE GROUND; IT OPENED AND A MUMMY CAME OUT. HE WAS VERY TALL AND WHITE. HE WAS HAVING A BLUE SWORD IN HIS HAND.

HE SAID, 'QUEBRAHMO.' WHICH MEANS HOW ARE YOU IN MUMMY'S LANGUAGE. THIS JAMES KNEW BECAUSE HE READ IT IN THE MUMMY'S BOOK BUT HE WAS JUST ABLE TO READ IT A LITTLE ONLY BECAUSE IT WAS BURNED IN THE FIRE.

THE MUMMIES WERE TALKING VERY MUCH. THE ONLY THING JAMES UNDERSTOOD WAS THAT HIS NAME WAS ALEX AND HE WAS THEIR HEAD. ALEX TOLD THEM TO ATTACK AND IN 10MINUTES EVERY ONE WAS DEAD.

JAMES WAS NOT ABLE TO SEE NOW THE DEAD AND HE THOUGHT TO DO SOMETHING. SO HE TOOK 1L OF POISON AND MIXED IT WITH OTHER CHEMICALS. HE KEPT ITS NAME BURHIMR. JAMES SAT IN A PLANE AND WENT WHERE THE MUMMIES WERE GOING AND THEN HE THREW IT ON THE MUMMIES BUT NOTHING HAPPENED. THEY SAW HIS PLANE AND THEY STARTED FLYING AND THEY JUMPED ON HIS PLANE. JAMES QUICKLY TOOK HIS PARASUIT AND JUMPED FROM THE WINDOW SO HE DID NOT GET ONE SCRATCH ALSO.

JAMES RAN VERY FAST AND TOOK ANOTHER PLANE AND CROSSED AMERICA. JAMES CAME IN HIS LAB AND STARTED SEEING THEM AND THEN HE SAW THAT THE MUMMIES WERE SMELLING THE PATH; THEY WERE COMING TOWARDS HIS LAB, HE THOUGHT TO CHANGE THE PLACE.

BUT HE SAW CHRISTINO DAVID. JAMES CALLED HIM INSIDE HIS LAB AND HE SAID THAT YOU WANT TO KILL ME. CHRISTINO SAID THAT YES, I WANT TO KILL YOU AND THAT BOMB, THAT RC POWDER AND THAT POISON WAS ALL DONE BY ME. JAMES SAID THAT YOU WANTED TO KILL ME NOW I WOULD KILL YOU AND THAT TO BADLY. HE SAID THAT KILL ME. JAMES SAID, 'DIE.' AND HE STARTED BEATING HIM A LOT AND THEN CHRISTINO SAID THAT YOU SHOULD KILL ME WITH YOUR GUN AND. JAMES SAID THAT OK, YOUR LAST WISH WOULD BE FULFILLED AND HE TOOK HIS GUN AND AS HE WAS GOING TO KILL HIM, JAMES HEARD A KNOCK. HE OPENED IT AND HE SAW ALEX AND THE OTHERS WERE DESTROYING THE FOREST.

ALEX HELD HENRYS' NECK AND THREW HIM HE QUICKLY TOOK HIS COMPRESSOR AND PUT IT IN HIS POCKET. THEN HE TURNED AND HE SAW THAT ALEX WAS STANDING BACK OF HIM. JAMES THREW HIM AND HE QUICKLY TOOK HIS GUN AND HE SHOT HIM WITH HIS ALL THE BULLETS BUT NOTHING HAPPENED. ALEX CAME AND HE HELD HENRY'S NECK AND BANGED HIM WITH THE TABLE. JAMES JUMPED, CURLED HIS LEG AND HAND AND BANGED WITH THE WINDOW AND CAME OUT. AND THAT WAS HIS VERY BIG AND LAST MISTAKES SINCE THERE WERE 1000 OF MUMMIES WERE WAITING FOR HIM. ONE MUMMY PICKED HIS HEAD AND STARTED BEATING HIM ON HIS STOMACH AND THEN HE BEAT HIM VERY TIGHTLY ON HIS MOUTH AND HE WENT TOWARDS ALEX FLYING. ALEX PICKED HIM UP AND SAID SOMETHING AND SUDDENLY ALL THE MUMMIES COME IN A LINE AND THEN HE THREW HIM IN THAT LINE; THEY STARTED BEATING HIM WITH THEIR LEGS.

JAMES TOOK OUT HIS FAINTER AND HE FAINTED HIMSELF SO THAT HE FEELS

LESS HURT. ALEX BEAT HE WITH GLASS BOTTLES AND HE WAS AGAIN CONSCIOUS. JAMES QUICKLY GOT UP AND RAN TO THE RIVER. HE TOOK OUT HIS MOTORBOAT AND RAN. AFTER SOMETIME HE TOOK AN AIRPLANE AND HE WENT TO INDIA. OVER THERE HE BOOKED A ROOM IN AGRA. NO ONE WAS KNOWING THIS NEWS LEAVING AMERICANS AND EGYPT'S PEOPLE AND THEY WERE DEAD LEAVING HENRY. THEY DID NOT KNOW BECAUSE MUMMIES HAD BROKEN TRANSFORMERS AND EMP AND WITH THEIR POWER ALSO THEY HAD DONE SOMETHING.

JAMES WAS SITTING IN HIS ROOM THINKING ABOUT HOW TO DEFEAT THEM AND THEN HE HEARD PEOPLE SHOUTING, HE WENT TO SEE WHAT WAS GOING ON AND WHEN HE OPENED THE GATE ALEX WAS STANDING AND HE WAS WAITING FOR HIM. WHEN ALEX WAS STANDING THAT TIME ONLY JAMES GOT AN IDEA TO GO TO M.R OCKWILL. M.R OCKWILL WAS AN ONLY WIZARD IN THE COUNTRY AND HE WAS IN AGRA.

HE QUICKLY CLOSED THE GATE BUT HE BROKE IT. HE BEAT HIM ON THE STOMACH, THEN ON HIS FACE AND THEN HE BEAT HIM SO TIGHTLY THAT HE WENT FLYING AND HE BANGED WITH THE WALL. HE PICKED A TABLE AND HE THREW IT ON HIM. HE TOOK SOME BOTTLES AND BANGED WITH HIM. JAMES THOUGHT THAT HE IS NO LONGER SAFE HERE SO HE THOUGHT TO JUMP FROM THE WINDOW. AND NOTHING MUCH WOULD HAPPEN TO HIM BECAUSE HE IS ON THE 1ST FLOOR.

JAMES JUMPED AND LANDED ON THE EARTH AND HE QUICKLY TOOK A CAR WHICH HE FOUND AND HE SAT IN IT AND DROVE AT 250KMPH SPEED. HE WAS HAVING THE KEY BECAUSE THE KEY WAS IN THE CAR ONLY. ALEX ALSO CAME BACK OFF HIM BUT THEN THE HOTEL'S BUILDING FELL ON HIM. JAMES WENT STRAIGHT TO M.R. OCKWILL. AS HE REACHED TO M.R OCKWILL HIS TIRE PUNCHER AND THEN HE WENT TO HIS HOUSE.

JAMES OPENED THE GATE AND HIS SERVANT CAME. A BOY LOOKING LIKE A SON OF A RICH MAN CAME OUT. HE SAID

THAT M.R OCKWILL IS NOT AT HOME AND HE IS IN HIS LAB NEAR TAJ MAHAL. SO JAMES TOOK A CYCLE AND STARTED CYCLING AND SOON IT BECAME VERY DARK. COLD WINDS WERE BLOWING. IT WAS RAINING BADLY. EVERYONE WAS RUNNING HERE AND THERE. MANY WERE DEAD.

WHEN JAMES WAS CYCLING, HE SAW MUMMIES. THEY PICKED HIM UP AND THREW HIS CYCLE. THE MUMMY PICKED HIM UP AND THREW HIM ON THE EARTH. HE WAS BADLY INJURED. HE SAW THAT ALEX AND HIS COMPANION CAME TOGETHER AND SAID SOME WORDS AND IT STARTED RAINING MORE HEAVILY AND FROM SKY A MAN CAME. THE WIND STARTED HOWLING. IT BECAME LIKE TORNADO. JAMES WAS NOT ABLE TO SEE ANYTHING. THE DUST WAS GOING IN HIS EYES SO HE CLOSED HIS EYES. HIS LEATHER JACKET WITH WHITE STRIPS ON THE BORDER WAS FLYING. THE HURT ON HIS HEAD BECAME DEEPER AND MORE BLOOD WAS COMING FROM HIS HEAD. HIS BLUE EYES WERE FULL OF TEARS. HIS WHITE FACE WAS

FULL OF DUST. THE WIND STOPPED. TO
HIS SURPRISE SOMEONE WAS STANDING.
HE WAS WEARING A LONG BLACK HOOD.
HIS FACE WAS NOT ABLE TO BE SEEN
BECAUSE HE WAS HAVING NO FACE. HIS
FACE WAS LIKE SHADOW. HE LOOKED
LIKE A REAL DEVIL. ANYONE CAN BE
AFRAID OF HIM. HE SAID SOMETHING
AND THE MUMMIES STARTED TALKING
IN ENGLISH. THE MUMMIES BEND THEIR
HEAD TO GIVE REGRET. HIS NAME WAS
SATEN. JAMES REMEMBERED THAT THIS
ONLY NAME M.R ROLED SAID IN THE SHIP.
THEY WERE SAYING LORD SATEN. SATEN
WAS VERY TALL AND THIN. JAMES GOT TO
KNOW THAT SOMETHING VERY WEIRD IS
GOING TO HAPPEN ON EARTH. 'THE BLACK
MAGIC,' SAID SATEN. THAT'S YOUR LAST
BREATHE REDSCOUT, SATEN SHOUTED.
HE LAUGHED LIKE A DEVIL. HE HELD
ONE MUMMIES NECK AND THREW HIM.
HE MADE HIS ON FINGER IN FRONT AND
ANOTHER BACK AND THEN HE CURLED IT;
A GOBLET CAME FROM THE GROUND.

HE SAID SOMETHING AND A BLUE
LINE CAME AND HE CUT A FINGER OF A

MUMMY; HE MIXED IT IN THE GOBLET. HE SAID SOMETHING AND ALL THE MUMMIES CHANGED INTO SPIRITS WHICH WERE VERY HUNGRY FOR DEATH. WHERE IS THAT MAN, WHERE IS HE? ALL THE SPIRITS POINTED AT HENRY. SATEN TURNED AND SAID, 'JAMES COOK. 'JAMES SAID TO HIM 'WHO ARE YOU AND HOW YOU KNOW MY NAME?

WHO DOESN'T KNOW YOUR AND MY NAME? HE WENT A LITTLE FAR AND SHOWED LIKE HE WAS NOT SEEING HENRY. I WANT TO KILL YOU BUT I CAN'T. HE TURNED AT JAMES AND CAME TOWARDS HIM. BUT I CAN KILL YOU HALF! SATEN RAISED HIS BOTH THE HAND WITH GREAT FORCE. ALL THE DIRT ON THE GROUND ROSE IN AIR. NOTHING WAS ABLE TO BE SEEN. WHEN THE DUST WENT, THE SPIRITS WERE NO LONGER THERE. SATEN RAISED HIS HAND.

JAMES RAISED IN THE AIR AND STARTED SHOUTING, HELP, HELP, AUUU, AAUUUEEE. HE DID HIS HAND DOWN AND JAMES CAME DOWN. SATEN STARTED TO THROW BLUE BALLS TOWARDS HENRY.

JAMES JUMPED AND JUMPED, HE
RAN AND RAN HE REACHED NEAR THE
GOBLET BUT AS HE WAS GOING TO JUMP,
HE CRASHED WITH THE GOBLET. SATEN
THREW A FIREBALL ON WHICH ICE WAS
THERE LIKE A STRIP. AS IT TOUCHED
HENRY, JAMES FLEW INTO THE AIR AND
FELL WITH A GREAT THUD. SATEN SAID
SOMETHING AND JAMES ROSE IN AIR. HIS
BODY STARTED ACHING.

HE SHOUTED VERY MUCH WITH PAIN
BUT NO ONE WAS THERE TO HELP. HE DID
HIS HAND DOWN AND JAMES FELL ON THE
GROUND. HE RAISED JAMES A BIT FROM
HIS POWER AND THREW HIM TOWARDS
THE GOBLET. HE MADE A WALL THERE
AND ATTACHED HIM IN IT. SATEN SAID
SOME BROKEL AND HIS BODY AGAIN
STARTED ACHING. IT WAS BETTER THAT
HE DIE. HIS BODY WAS ACHING LIKE 1000S
OF BULLETS HAD SHOT HIM.

IT WAS LIKE 100 OF KNIVES WERE
STABLED IN HIS STOMACH. IT WAS LIKE
THAT HE WAS HAVING OPERATION. BUT
HE COULDN'T DO ANYTHING BUT SHOUT. HE
SHOUTED VERY SLOWLY AND HIS SHOUT

WAS DECREASING WITH PAIN. HE WAS DYING WITH PAIN. SATEN WAS LAUGHING. SOON JAMES BECAME UNCONSCIOUS.

AFTER 9 HOURS JAMES AGAIN GOT CONSCIOUS. HE WAS HANDCUFFED IN THE WALL. HE TRIED TO MOVE IN FRONT AND HE MOVED ALSO 1METER. HE STRETCHED HIS HANDS AND THE CHAIN BROKE BUT THIS WAS NOT THE CASE WITH LEG ONE. OVER THERE ONLY 2 METER FAR FROM HIM WAS A KNIFE AND WHEN HE SAW IN THE FRONT, A BLUE BALL WAS SHINING IN THE DARK. IT WAS MID OF NIGHT. BUT WHEN JAMES LOOKED TOWARDS HIS WATCH, HE SAW THAT IT WAS BEING 5:30AM.

HE WANTED TO TAKE THE BIG BALL AND GET OUT OF THE CHAIN. HE LAY ON THE GROUND BUT THE KNIFE WAS PRETTY FAR. JAMES GOT UP AND TOOK OUT HIS JACKET. HE LAY ON THE GROUND AND TRIED TO TAKE THE KNIFE. AFTER 5 MINUTES, THE KNIFE WAS WITH HIM. HE MADE HIMSELF FREE AND WENT TOWARDS THE BALL. AS HE TOUCHED IT, HE ROSE IN THE AIR AND FELL ON THE GROUND. HE HAD GOT A MESSAGE. IT

SAID THERE ARE SOME PEOPLE IN THE WORLD WHO ARE BORN WITH GOD GIFTED POWERS. THESE POWERS ARE CALLED BROKEL. THEY HAVE THE SPECIAL POWERS TO DO MAGIC. NOT ACTUALLY MAGIC BUT A BOOKS NAME. THERE ARE BOOKS AND THEY HAVE VERY WEIRD AND SENSELESS NAMES. ALL THE BOOKS IN THE WORLD HAVE MAXIMUM 4 PAGES ON WHICH ABOUT THE BOOK IS WRITTEN. THE MAGICAL BOOK 'STRAYED' IS ABOUT WHAT YOU THINK THAT WILL HAPPEN TO YOUR OPPONENT. STRAYED ONLY SUPPORTS THE IMPOSSIBLE BROKEL BUT IT IS ONE OF THE TOUGHEST BROKEL IN THE WORLD. TWO PEOPLE HAVE TO SAY A BROKEL AND FROM THERE CORD (IT IS A BIG THING MADE OUT OF WOOD, SILVER, GOLD AND SPECIAL DIAMONDS ARE PUT ON IT TO HOLD THE CORD SO THAT IT DOESN'T BREAK) A BLUE OR RED OR GREEN OR ANY COLOR LINE CAME OUT AND AT LAST WHOSE BROKEL IS BETTER WINS AND WHAT THE BOOK IS ABOUT, DO THAT THING. FOR THIS SPECIAL PEOPLE THERE ARE SPECIAL SCHOOLS UNDERGROUND.

THERE ARE TWO SCHOOLS WITH SAME NAME AND IT IS REDSCOUT. JAMES WAS ALSO A MEMBER OF REDSCOUT AND HE IS VERY POWERFUL IN IT. SATEN IS THE MOST POWERFUL MAN BUT HE USED THE POWER IN BAD THINGS. SATEN WANTED TO KILL JAMES BUT JAMES CAME ON EARTH WITH THE HELP OF THE HEADMASTER.

JAMES WAS NOT ABLE TO BELIEVE ANYTHING BUT HE HAD TO BECAUSE ALL WHAT WAS HAPPENING WAS MAGIC. HE PINCHED HIMSELF TO SEE THAT HE WAS NOT DREAMING BUT IT WAS REAL. HE HAS TO SAVE THE WORLD SO HE TOOK HIS CYCLE AND WENT TOWARDS TAJ MAHAL. AFTER SOMETIME HE REACHED TO M.R. OCKWILL'S HOUSE. BUT ALAS! THERE WAS A BIG LOCK ON THE DOOR. JAMES SAT DOWN ON A BENCH AND STARTED CRYING. IT WAS 7:47AM. HE CRIED FOR LONG AND THEN HE SLEPT.

AFTER AN HOUR HE WOKE UP WITH THE NOISE OF PEOPLE SHOUTING. HE WOKE UP TO SEE. HE SAW SATEN. SATEN STARTED DOING BROKEL. HE MADE A BIG BALL AND THREW IT TOWARDS

HENRY. IT BANGED JAMES AND HE FELL FAR. SATEN TOOK OUT HIS CORD AND STARTED DOING BROKEL. NYCRUFRIST, VINGADFOM, STRATOSTIONG, FDECK, AND THE LAST HEUMOSTIAN. THIS ENTIRE BROKEL SATEN SAID WHEN JAMES WAS ON THE FLOOR. THIS BROKEL WERE NOT POWERFUL SO HE GOT UP.

SATEN CAME AND PICKED JAMES FROM HIS NECK. HE STARTED STRANGLING HIM. HE THOUGHT HE WAS VERY NEAR TO DEATH AND AFTER 1 HOUR HE WOULD BE IN REDSCOUT. THAT TIME ONLY THERE WAS A BANG AND M.R OCKWILL WAS STANDING BACK OF SATEN. HE MADE SATEN FALL AND A CAR CAME, THEY TOOK HIM SOMEWHERE UNKNOWN.

SATEN GOT UP AND SAID SOME BROKEL, HE THREW A BIG ROCK AT HENRY. JAMES JUMPED FROM THERE SO HE WAS SAVED. SATEN SAID MULASCLE, A BUILDING STARTED FALLING ON HENRY. HE STARTED RUNNING AS FAST AS HE COULD AND WHEN IT WAS GOING COMPLETELY, JAMES DID A FLIP AND CAME IN THE MID OF A BRIDGE. SATEN SAID SOME BROKEL AND THE FIRST

STRING OF THE BRIDGE BROKE. JAMES LOOKED BACK AND STARTED RUNNING AND RUNNING AND WHEN HE WAS GOING TO CROSS IT THE SECOND ALSO BROKE. WHEN HE HAD CROSSED ¾ OF THE BRIDGE AND JUST ONE METER WAS LEFT; THE FOURTH STRING BROKE. JAMES WAS IN THE AIR, MOVING HIS HANDS AND LEGS RAPIDLY. HE FELL BUT HE PUT HIS LEGS SOMEHOW WITH GREAT FORCE ON THE LAND AND LIKE A SPRING HE JUMPED AND HE FELL WITH A THUD ON THE LAND SATEN SAID 'VONDRIST SIOPER.'

A HOUSE FELL ON HIM BUT HE WAS AGAIN SAVED. HE SAID, 'GIODER.' HE TOOK A DOOR AND MADE A HOVER BOAT; HE THREW AT HIM. JAMES JUMPED INTO THE AIR AND LANDED ON THE HOVER BOAT. SATEN STARTED CHASING HIM.

HE TOOK A SWORD AND HE CUT HENRY'S HOVER BOAT. HE TOOK THE HOVER BOAT AND STARTED CHASING HIM. FROM HIS POWER HE PICKED UP A CAN AND HE THREW AT HENRY. JAMES TURNED HIS FACE SO HE WAS SAVED. HE PICKED UP

SOME WOODS AND THREW AT HIM. HE BEND HIS BODY SO HE WAS SAVED.

SATEN SAID 'LING LONG LEAST.' AND ALL THINGS WHICH WERE ON THE GROUND FLEW INTO THE AIR AND STARTED TO BANG WITH HENRY. HE WAS TRYING TO SAVE HIMSELF BUT A BIG ROCK HIT HIS HOVER BOARD AND IT BROKE; HE FELL ON THE LAND. JAMES JUMPED INTO THE AIR AND CAME ON HIS HOVER BOAT. SATEN SAW HIM AND HE ALSO JUMPED ON HIS HOVER BOAT. WHEN JAMES GOT UP HE DID NOT KNOW THAT SATEN IS ALSO THERE WITH HIM.

HE GOT A SHOCK. SATEN PUT HIS HAND ON HIS FACE AND HE STARTED STOPPING HIS BREATHE. WHEN THEY WERE GOING JAMES SAW A WOOD, HE QUICKLY PICKED IT UP AND HE BEAT IT ON SATEN'S FACE AND HE LEFT HIM. HE THREW HIM ON HIS HOVER BOAT.

YOU KNOW THE MEANING OF FOOL? I WILL TELL YOU. FOOL MEANS YOU. YOU THINK THAT THEY WERE MUMMIES. NO THEY WERE NOT. THEY WERE DEATHLY SPIRITS.

DEATHLY SPIRITS YOU KNOW, THEY ARE THE SPIRITS WHO ARE SEARCHING FOR DEATH. THEIR WORK IS JUST TO KILL. THE MISSION OF THEIR LIFE IS DEATH. AND THEY WILL KILL YOU. YOU REMEMBER ABOUT YOUR FRIENDS. JAMES SAID, 'NO.' SATEN SAID, 'I WILL MAKE YOU REMEMBER.' YOUR FRIEND ROELD AND HALEN. ROELD CAN MAKE ANYTHING ALIVE AND HALEN WHO HAS STILL NOT LEARNED BUT SHE HAS THE CAPACITY. YOU THINK THAT ALL WAS DONE BY CHRISTINO. YOU ARE CORRECT BUT I SEND HIM TO KILL YOU.

LAPASCO WAS ALSO SENT BY ME. THE CRUISE LINER CAME SO THAT YOU ARE DEAD BY MY HANDS.

THE OWNER WAS ALSO SENT BY ME. THE MUSEUM OWNER WAS ALSO SEND BY ME. THIS ALL I DID BECAUSE I WANTED TO COME BACK TO LIFE AND THIS WAS ONLY MY DEVICE. AND YOU THINK THAT THE HURRICANE WAS IN REAL. NO IT WAS JUST A RUMOR. IT WAS NOT A GLASS, IT WAS JUST A RUMOR. THE BROKEL WAS REALLY DONE BY HIM BUT IT WAS NOT

REAL HURRICANE. YOU WERE FIRST A BEGGAR. I CALLED YOU IN THE FOREST AND I MADE YOU GENIUS SO THAT YOU GET AN IDEA TO MAKE ELIXIR. SO THAT YOU CAN TEST IT ON THE MUMMIES. THE MUSEUM OWNER CHANGED THE BOXES AS HE WAS SEND BY ME.

THEY WERE SPIRITS IN THE MUMMIES FORM. YOU MADE THEM ALIVE AND NOTHING WOULD HAVE HAPPENED IF YOU WOULD HAVE GIVEN THEM WC POWDER. THE MUMMIES MADE ALEX ALIVE AND ALEX MADE ME. INDIRECTLY YOU MADE ME ALIVE. I WANT TO KILL YOU AND DESTROY THE REDSCOUT. AFTER SAYING THESE WORDS HE SAID SOME BROKEL AND FROM HIS HAND A BLUE LINE CAME AND HIT HIM.

JAMES FLEW INTO THE AIR AND LANDED ON THE EARTH WITH A JERK. HE THOUGHT HE WAS VERY NEAR TO DEATH. DEATH AND DEATH WAS GOING IN HIS MIND. SATEN CAME TOWARDS HIM. HE PICKED HIM UP AND STARTED BEATING ON HIS STOMACH. THEN HE BEAT HIM ON HIS FACE. SATEN CAME TOWARDS HIM. HE

TRIED TO GO BACK BUT HE HELD HIS NECK AND PICKED HIM UP AND SAID THIS WOULD BE YOUR LAST BREATHE. YOU WOULD BE SOON IN REDSCOUT WITH YOUR FRIENDS, AS NOTHING IS CHANGED BECAUSE YOU WERE ON EARTH FOR 1 YEAR BUT ONE YEAR OF EARTH IS FIVE MONTHS IN REDSCOUT. HE TOOK OUT HIS KNIFE AND AS HE WAS GOING TO STABLE IT ALEX COME AND HELD HIS HAND.

SATEN SHOUTED ANGRILY, 'HOW DARE YOU TO HOLD MY HAND!!!!!!!!??????, I WILL KILL YOU!!!!!!' SATEN SAID SOME WORDS AND ALEX WAS BADLY INJURED. ALEX WAS SAYING MASTER, MASTER LEAVE ME DON'T KILL ME IN A CRYING TONE. SATEN MADE HIS LEFT ARM RED AND HE BEAT HIM ON HIS FACE. SATEN CAME IN FRONT AND SAID THAT I WILL FEEL NICE TO KILL YOU. HE BEAT HIM WITH HIS HEAD AND ALEX WAS DEAD. HE CAME TOWARDS JAMES AND BEAT HIM AND HE FAINTED.

Hᴇ ᴡᴀꜱ ꜱᴏᴍᴇᴡʜᴇʀᴇ ɪɴ ᴜɴᴋɴᴏᴡɴ PLACE. JAMES WOKE UP AND SAW THAT HE WAS IN PRISON. HE WENT AND HE HELD THE BARS AND HE SHOUTED 'WHO IS THIS, LEAVE ME.' BUT NO ONE CAME. JAMES SAT IN A CORNER AND STARTED CRYING. HE SAW THAT A MAN WAS COMING. HE HAD A HUNTER WITH HIM. AS HE ENTERED IN THE PRISON, JAMES HELD HIS HAND AND ROLLED IT. HE PICKED HIM UP ON HIS BACK; THREW HIM. HE FELL ON THE MAN WITH GREAT FORCE.

HE PICKED HIM UP AND STARTED BEATING HIM ON HIS STOMACH. HE TOOK

THE KEY FROM THE MAN AND AS HE WAS GOING TO OPEN ANOTHER MAN CAME. HE HELD THAT MAN'S NECK FROM THE BARS AND STARTED KILLING HIM. THEY BOTH WERE DEAD. HE CAME OUT OF HIS PRISON AND STARTED RUNNING. AS HE WAS GOING TO COME OUT A BIG DOOR MADE OF STEEL COVERED THE WHOLE PLACE. JAMES GOT TO KNOW THAT THERE WAS NO WAY TO COME OUT SO HE WENT BACK. JAMES WAS FEELING LIKE HE IS A JINX. THE PRISON WAS A DARK PLACE. IT WAS ACTUALLY NOT A PLACE BUT A DONJON.

THERE WAS A DIRTY AND RUBY BED WITH A WASHROOM BESIDE IT. IT WAS AS SMALL AS HALF OF A SMALL ROOM. THE BAD SMELL WAS ALL OVER THE PLACE MAKING JAMES BLOCK HIS NOSE.

HE COULD HARDLY WAIT. JAMES THOUGHT TO SEARCH FOR HIS COMPUTER. SOON HIS BOTH THE HANDS WERE IN THE POCKET OF THE JEANS AND THE LEATHER JACKET. BUT HE COULD NOT FIND IT. HE COLLAPSED IN THE DIRTY BED AND PILLOW. HE LAID DOWN ON IT AND STARTED THINKING. THEN HE REMEMBERED THAT

HE HAD KEPT HIS ALL THE THINGS IN A DENIM BAG. HE LOOKED DOWN AND THERE WAS HIS BAG UNDER THE BED HE TOOK OUT IS COMPRESSOR FROM IT. HE OPENED HIS COMPUTER AND STARTED WATCHING IT. HE OPENED HIS COMPRESSOR AND STARTED SEEING SATEN. HE WAS ABLE TO SEE HIM BECAUSE WHEN SATEN WAS GOING TO KILL HENRY, HE QUIETLY STUCK THE CAMERA IN HIS HOOD. HE SAW THAT SATEN WAS IN A PALACE.

HE SAID, 'UHPHORISO' AND ALL THE GUARDS FLEW IN THE AIR AND THEN THEY DIED. SATEN WENT INSIDE AND ANOTHER PERSON CAME WITH A SWORD.

SATEN HELD HIS SWORD AND WITH A LITTLE PRESSURE HE PUSHED HIS SWORD AND HE FLEW IN THE AIR. AFTER THAT A GROUP OF GUARDS CAME WITH SWORDS AND GUNS. SATEN TOOK OUT HIS CORD AND SAID, 'MILOE AVACUSA'AND HE FLEW A LITTLE IN THE AIR AND ALL THE GUNS AND SWORD ALSO FLEW IN THE AIR, THE GUNS STARTED KILLING THERE MASTER AND IT WAS SAME WITH THE SWORD. SOME MORE PEOPLE CAME WITH SOMETHING

WHICH WAS MADE BY WOOD AND STEEL WAS ATTACHED ON THE END. SATEN SAID, 'XCRAM' AND THEY ALL DIED, THEN MANY MORE CAME, THEY ALSO DIED. THIS NEWS WENT TO THE KING. THE KING ORDERED TO CLOSE ALL THE GATES. BUT AS SATEN CAME NEAR THE FIRST GATE.

HE TOOK OUT HIS CORD AND SAID, 'STRAYEDOTWO' AND A BANG, THE GATE OPENED. AS IT OPENED, THE MACHINEGUN STARTED SHOOTING HIM.

HE SAID, 'SYOPERED' AND ALL THE BULLETS STOPPED AND IT HIT THEM THEN THEY DIED. WHILE HE WAS KILLING OTHERS THE SECRET GATE OPENED. A VERY BIG REGIMENT OF ARMY CAME. THEY WERE HOLDING VERY HARD AND FAT STEEL IN THEIR HAND. THE STEEL WAS ENGRAVED WITH DIAMONDS. MIRROR WAS ALSO THERE. THEY SAT DOWN, AND THEY PUT THEIR STEEL PROTECTION FRONT OF THEM AND THEN THEY PUT THEIR STEEL PROTECTION ON THEIR HEAD. THEN A MAN WAS THERE SANDING VERY FAR. SATEN SAID 'RIOTRISM' FROM HIS CORD A BLUE THING CAME AND IT

HIT THE PROTECTION OF STEEL. THE MAN STANDING SHOUTED '1PRO 'THEY TOOK OUT ANOTHER STEEL PROTECTION AND THEN THEY TOOK OUT ANOTHER AND ANOTHER AND ANOTHER AND ANOTHER AND ANOTHER AND THEY MADE THEIR STEEL PROTECTION IN FRONT OF SATEN'S POWER AND BROKEL STOPPED. A MAN CAME WITH HIS PROTECTION AND A SWORD AND HE TOOK SATEN'S CORD AND HE BROKE IT. HE WENT BACK TO HIS PLACE. SATEN LOOKED VERY ANGRY. HE SAID, 'GO DIE.' HE TOOK OUT HIS CORD, A VERY STRONG BROKEL CAME AND HIT THEM. THEY AGAIN STARTED DOING THAT ONLY, BUT AS THEY DID, THE BROKEL BROKE THE PROTECTION BADLY AND EVERYONE DIED, EVEN THAT MAN ALSO. HE WENT ANGRILY TO THE KING. HE OPENED THE DOOR.

HE KILLED EVERY ONE AND HE WENT TO A PERSON HE ASKED HIM; WHERE IS THE KING? THAT MAN SAID VERY SCARE FULLY THAT GO RIGHT AND THEN LEFT, THEN SATEN KILLED HIM. HE WENT STRAIGHT TO THE KING. HE OPENED

THE DOOR; HE KILLED THE PEOPLE WHO WERE PRESENT WITH THE KING. HE WENT TO THE KING. HE HELD HIS NECK AND HE BROKE THE THRONE ON WHICH HE WAS SITTING. HE THREW HIM ON THE FLOOR. HE SAID THAT I WOULD NOT KILL YOU WITH BROKEL. HE WENT TOWARDS HIM AND HE BEAT HIM WITH HIS LEG. HE PICKED HIM UP AND BEAT HIM WITH HIS HAND ON HIS STOMACH. HE TOOK HIM AND BANGED HIM WITH THE WALL. HE PICKED A TABLE AND HE THREW IT ON HIM. HE TOOK A SWORD AND HE STABLED IN IT. HE TOOK HIM TO THE BALCONY AND HE THREW HIM FROM IT.

HE SAID NOW I AM THE KING AND HE LAUGHED AND FROM HIS POWER HE MADE AGAIN PROGRAMS COME ON THE T.V AND AGAIN THE E.M.P CAME. HE SHOUTED THAT 'NOW I AM THE KING AND IF ANY ONE TRIES TO DEFEAT ME, HE HAS TO ALSO SUFFER LIKE THIS KING. JAMES GOT A SHOCK. SATEN TOOK OUT THE CAMERA WHICH HE HAD FIT ON HIS BACK AND THEN HE CAUGHT A PERSON AND SAID HIM TO DO HIS ONE WORK AND THE WORK WAS

TO TELL ALL THE WORLD ABOUT THAT HE HAD BECOME THE KING, HE GAVE HIM THE CAMERA AND THE MAN GAVE TO THE REPORTER, IN 1 HOUR EVERYONE WAS KNOWING ABOUT IT. THE DEATHLY SPIRITS WERE SOMEWHERE HIDDEN AND JAMES COULDN'T SEE ONE OF THEM ALSO THEN.

JAMES WAS LOST OF WORDS. HE WANTED TO DIE. THE UGLY TRUTH WAS IN FRONT OF HIM THAT HE WILL NOT BE ALIVE AFTER 1 OR 2 HOUR. HE KNEW THAT PEOPLE WOULD COME IN THE PRISON AND KILL HIM. HE CAME OUT OF HIS PRISON. HE LEANED TOWARDS A WALL AND STARTED CRYING. HE WAS OBVIOUSLY VERY SAD. BUT WHAT COULD HE DO. HE THOUGHT ABOUT M.R OCKWILL. WHERE WOULD HAVE HE WENT.

IT MIGHT BE THAT HE IS IN THIS AREA ONLY. HE SAT DOWN ON THE FLOOR AND STARTED TO MAKE THE BED FOR HIM TO SLEEP. HE LAY DOWN ON HIS BED AND HE WAS SO TIRED THAT HE SLEPT IN A MOMENT.

IT WAS PAST 12. JAMES HEARD A SOUND. HE QUICKLY GOT UP IN FEAR. COME JAMES COME ALONG WITH ME. I WILL TAKE OUT FROM THE MAZE. JAMES LEAPT INTO THE AIR AS HE WAS KETHLAN OCKWILL. HE CAME OUT OF THE PRISON AND HUGGED HIM.

WHERE WERE YOU? IN THE PRISON. SO HOW YOU CAME OUT? THE STORY IS VERY COMPLICATED.

ANYWAY NOW WE HAVE TO COME OUT OF THIS IRON WALL. THAT'S IMPOSSIBLE. NOTHING IS IMPOSSIBLE. SEE, THE DOOR CLOSES WHEN YOU CROSS 50METRE AND 1 METER IS LEFT. THE SPEED OF THE DOOR WHEN IT IS GOING TO CLOSE IS BY RUNNING. HOW MUCH YOUR SPEED WILL BE, THAT MUCH FAST IT WILL CLOSE. I HAVE A MEASURING TAPE WITH ME. FIRST WE WILL GO VERY SLOWLY AND WHEN JUST ON METER IS LEFT WE WILL LEARN SLIDE BY LEANING THE WALL. THEY WALKED AS SLOWLY AS THEY COULD. KETHLAN WAS HOLDING A MEASURING TAPE WITH HIM. WHEN 50 METER WAS OVER THEY TOOK THE SPEED. AS THEY RAN THE

DOOR STARTED CLOSING SLOWLY. AS IT WAS GOING TO CLOSE, JAMES PASSED HIS BAG AND HE SLID DOWN THE DOOR WITH M.R OCKWILL. THEY KEPT ON GOING FROM THE TRAPDOORS BY THIS PROCESS.

THEY HAD CROSSED 3 DOORS AND NOW IT WAS THE FOURTH ONE. AS THEY ENTERED, THEY SAW THAT 3 GUARDS WERE THERE HOLDING GUNS. I WOULD TAKE ON THEM BOTH AND YOU, M.R OCKWILL GO ON THAT ONE. JAMES RAN LIKE A CAT AND STOOD BEHIND THE GUARDS. HE KNOCKED ON THEIR BACKS TO TAKE ATTENTION.

AS THEY LOOKED BACK, ONE OF THE GUARDS RELOADED HIS GUN. JAMES JUMPED AND TOOK THE BALANCE ON THE HAND OF THE GUARD. HE ROLLED HIMSELF ALONG WITH THE GUARD'S HAND. THE MAN SHOUTED IN PAIN. THE OTHER MAN RELOADED HIS GUN. THE MAN PRESSED THE TRIGGER. JAMES BEND HIS BODY AND THE BULLET SHOT THE OTHER GUARD.

HE CAME ON THE FLOOR. THE MAN TRIED TO SHOOT HIM AGAIN BUT HE

MISSED THE TARGET. JAMES WAS RUNNING VERY FAST AROUND THE WHOLE ROOM. HE PRESSED THE MAN'S NECK AND STUCK HIM ON THE WALL. HE MADE HIS RIGHT HAND ALSO STUCK IN THE WALL SO THAT HE SHOOTS IN THE RIGHT. JAMES TOOK THE GUARD'S GUN AND HE SHOT HIM.

ON THE OTHER HAND M.R OCKWILL WAS FIGHTING WITH THE GUARD WHO HAD NO GUN. HE PUNCHED HIM ON HIS FACE, ON HIS STOMACH AND SAT ON HIM TO PUNCH HIM ON HIS FACE. JAMES LOOKED TOWARDS M.R OCKWILL. IN MATTER OF SECONDS JAMES SHOT THE GUARD. THANKS. WELCOME. NOW YOU DO A PROMISE. WHICH TYPE OF PROMISE? PARENT'S PROMISE. BUT MY PARENTS ARE DEAD. THEY AREN'T.

YOU LEAVE THIS ALL AND DO A PROMISE THAT IF I AM DEAD THEN YOU WILL NOT COME TO HELP ME. I WILL. DON'T WORRY I WILL MEET YOU AGAIN BUT HOW. SEE JAMES I AM A TEACHER AT REDSCOUT. SO I WILL GO BACK TO REDSCOUT. WHERE ARE MY PARENTS? IN REDSCOUT. THEY ARE NOT DEAD. THEY

LIVE IN THE REDSCOUT COUNTRY. IT WAS
THE FIRST BEST NEWS HE HAD HEARD IN
HIS LIFE.

HE WAS SO HAPPY THAT HE COULDN'T
TELL. HE TRIED TO STOP HIS HAPPINESS.
LET'S MOVE FURTHER. PROMISE ME.
BUT FIRST YOU PROMISE ME THAT YOU
WILL MEET ME IN REDSCOUT. THEY BOTH
PROMISED EACH OTHER AND AT LAST
THEY CAME OUT. THEY DIDN'T SAW THAT
THERE WERE 10 TO 50 GUARDS STANDING.

THEY RAN AS FAST AS POSSIBLE
AND THEY CROSSED THE GATE. BUT
MEANWHILE M.R OCKWILL WAS DEAD.
JAMES LOOKED BACK TO HELP BUT THEN
HE REMEMBERED THE PROMISE. TEARS
ROLLED DOWN FROM HIS CHEEKS. HE RAN
OUT OF THE PLACE AND CAME INSIDE
A CAR.

IT WAS A DIRTY CAR. THE SEATS
WERE TORN. THE SPEED WAS ALSO
LESS. IT WAS FOUR SEATER CAR BUT THE
LUGGAGE HAD TAKEN THE BACK PLACE.
HE THOUGHT THAT FOOD MUST INSIDE IT,
SO HE COULD HAVE IT FOR HIM BECAUSE
HE HAD NEITHER EATEN FOOD NOR

WATER FOR DAYS. JAMES QUICKLY TOOK OUT HIS COMPRESSOR FROM HIS BAG. HE TOOK OUT A MACHINE GUN TO SHOOT THE GUARDS. HE PEEPED HIS HEAD OUT OF THE CAR'S WINDOW TO LOOK THE PLACE WHERE HE WAS.

IT WAS A ONE STORY HOUSE. IT WAS NOT PAINTED. IT WAS WHITE AND THE ROOF WAS DARK. THE GUARDS WERE RUNNING OUT OF THE PLACE. THEY STARTED SHOOTING TOWARDS HENRY'S CAR. HE CAME OUT AND CONTINUOUSLY SHOT ALL THE GUARDS. MORE GUARDS WERE COMING AND THE NUMBER WAS INCREASING. JAMES SAT IN THE CAR TURNED THE KEY AND TOOK THE TOP SPEED.

HE CAME IN A DENSE PLACE WHERE NO ONE LIVED BUT HE WAS WRONG. PEOPLE LIVED JUST BESIDE IT. HE THOUGHT TO STAY WITH A FAMILY FOR A DAY TO GET INFORMATION. HE WENT INSIDE A WHITE HOUSE WITH RED STRIPES. HE RANG THE

BELL. A VOICE CAME FROM INSIDE. WHO ARE YOU? I AM JAMES COOK, I THINK YOU KNOW ME.

REALLY. YES. A MAN OPENED THE DOOR. HE WAS HAVING A LONG FACE. HE HAD A DENSE MOUSTACHE AND A PALE FACE. HIS AGE MUST BE ABOVE 48 YEARS. HE GRANTED JAMES IN THE HOUSE. IT WAS NOT A BIG PLACE BUT IT WAS MUCH CLEAN. IN THE FRONT WAS THE KITCHEN. IN THE SIDE WAS A HALL AND IN LEFT THERE WERE TWO ROOMS. A STAIR LEAD TO THE NEXT FLOOR.

THERE WERE TWO ROOMS SIDE BY SIDE WHICH WERE BOTH GUEST'S ROOM. THEY HAD ONE CHILD. THE CHILD SLEPT IN HIS OWN ROOM AND THE PARENTS IN THE OTHER. IN THE KITCHEN, THERE WAS A CRACK ON THE FLOOR IT DIDN'T LOOK AS A CRACK. JAMES ASKED THE OWNER OF THE HOUSE ABOUT IT.

IT IS THE UNDERGROUND PLACE WHERE WE WASH CLOTHS AND KEEP OTHER THINGS. BUT NOW IT IS A PLACE FOR HIDING. HIS WIFE WAS A KIND HEARTED LADY. SHE WAS THIN AND WAS WEARING

A JACKET AND JEANS. SHE WAS ALSO HAVING A LONG FACE. SHE LOOKED LIKE A GIRL OF 19 TO 22 AGE BUT SHE WAS DOUBLE. THEIR CHILD WAS VERY SERIOUS. HE USED TO STAY IN HIS ROOM AND READ BOOKS. HE WAS SELDOM SEEN.

JAMES WAS GIVEN THE GUEST ROOM. JAMES ENTERED IN HIS ROOM. IT WAS A CLEAN ROOM. THERE WAS AN AC, TV, BOOKS TO READ AND MANY OTHER THINGS. HE OPENED TELEVISION. NO SHOW WAS COMING LEAVING NEWS. EVERY CHANNEL WAS SHOWING HOW SATEN IS KILLING PEOPLE AND OTHER THINGS WHICH HE KNEW.

THEY SHOWED HOW BADLY PEOPLE WERE KILLED. JAMES GOT UP AND WENT TOWARDS THE DOOR. 'WHERE ARE YOU GOING?' SAID THE LADY. SOMEWHERE ELSE? BUT AT LEAST HAVE THE LUNCH. THANK YOU, BUT I HAVE TO LEAVE. JAMES WENT OUT OF THE HOUSE AND THEN IN HIS CAR.

HE DROVE FOR 90 KM AND HE REACHED AN EMPTY PLACE. HE WAS IN SYDNEY. HE MADE HIS LAB AND WENT INSIDE IT. HE

THOUGHT TO EMPTY THE LUGGAGE. THERE
WAS A BIG TRUNK WHICH WAS SEALED
BY LEATHER BUT JAMES SOMEHOW
OPENED IT. THERE WERE MORE THAT
150 SHOTGUNS AND 500 HANDGUNS. THE
NEXT TRUNK WAS MUCH HEAVIER AND IT
WAS THRICE AS BIG AS THE FIRST TRUNK.
IT WAS HAVING 150 MACHINEGUNS. THE
NEXT TRUNK WAS HAVING LOTS AND
LOTS OF FOOD. THERE WERE CABBAGE,
TOMATO, POTATO, SPINACH, ONION, LEMON
AND MANY MORE VEGETABLES. THERE
WAS FOOD FOR 5 PEOPLE WHO COULD EAT
IT THRICE A DAY AND THEY WILL FINISH
IT AFTER 100 DAYS.

JAMES KEPT THE TRUNKS IN HIS
LAB AND PARKED THE CAR BACK OF HIS
LAB. HE LAY ON THE BED AND STARTED
THINKING HOW TO KILL SATEN. HE
THOUGHT TO CALL HIS 6 BEST FRIENDS.

HE MADE A CALL AND HE TOLD THEM
THE ADDRESS. WHEN HE CALLED THE
SIXTH FRIEND, HE GOT A BAD NEWS. HIS
SIXTH FRIEND WAS DEAD. WHAT A BAD
NEWS BUT NOW THEY HAVE TO FACE IT.
HIS FRIENDS ARRIVED AFTER 19 HOURS
BY AIRPLANE. THEY ALL HUGGED EACH
OTHER. SO FROM WHERE YOU GOT THIS

PLANE. STOLEN MAN. THEY ALL ENTERED IN THE LAB.

AS I KNOW THAT THE WORLD IS GOING TO BE DESTROYED. A MAN NAMED SATEN IS KILLING EVERYONE. SOON WE CAN ALSO COME IN THE LIST OF DEAD PEOPLE. JAMES SAID THAT WE HAD TO DEFEAT THEM, IS IT CLEAR? HIS FIFTH FRIEND RON CAME IN THE FRONT. HE WAS A HANDSOME LOOKING GUY. HE HAD GOLDEN HAIR. BLUE EYES AND POINTED NOSE. RONALD SAID SHOUTING 'IT IS BETTER WE DIE FROM THE HANDS OF SATEN BECAUSE BY CHANCE IF WE KILL THEN IT IS VERY DIFFICULT TO START THE NEW LIFE BECAUSE EVERYTHING IS DESTROYED AND WE WILL DIE BECAUSE OF HUNGER. WE WOULD NEVER BE ABLE TO KILL SATEN. HE HAS GOT MAGICAL POWERS AND WE DON'T HAVE THEM, HAVE WE? YES, I HAVE. IT IS BETTER THAT WE GO TOWARDS SATEN'S SIDE. AT LEAST WE WILL NOT BE KILLED. YOU WANT TO GO SO GO. I WILL. WHO WANT TO COME WITH ME? RAISE THEIR HANDS. NO ONE RAISED THEIR HAND. FINE! I GOT THE

ANSWER. AND WHAT WERE YOU SAYING? YOU WERE KIDDING. I WASN'T. 'OH, YOU HAVE MAGICAL POWERS' SAID RONALD SARCASTICALLY. YES, I HAVE. MEANS YOU WANT TO SAY YOU ARE ONE OF A KIND LIKE SATEN. YES. DON'T KID. I AM NOT KIDDING. YOU ARE A LIAR. I AM NOT. YOU ARE. ALBUS IS A LIAR. HOW YOU ARE FEELING ALBUS BY HAVING POWERS. SHUT UP, RONALD. I WON'T. IT'S NOT YOUR PLACE. THE LAB IS MINE. I WON'T GO FROM HERE. JAMES LOST HIS TEMPER.

HE WENT TOWARDS HIM AND GAVE HIM A TIGHT SLAP. RONALD KEPT ONE HAND ON HIS CHEEKS AND RAN TOWARDS HIM. THEY BOTH HELD EACH OTHER'S CALLER. THEY BEAT EACH OTHER ON THEIR HEAD, STOMACH AND FACE. JAMES HELD RON'S CALLER AND SAID THAT YOU ARE MAD AND YOU DON'T KNOW DYEING FROM HUNGER IS BETTER THAN DYING FROM THE HANDS OF A DEVIL. WATSON WHO LOOKED LIKE A CAT AND HAD A SHORT MOUSTACHE RAN TOWARDS THEM BOTH TO FREE THEM. JOHN AND WATSON HELD RONALD AND CHRIS TO HENRY. RONALD

WAS SHOUTING LIKE DINOSAURS AND ACTING LIKE A PRISONER. HE WAS TRYING TO GET RID OF THEM AND KILL HENRY.

WATSON GAVE A TIGHT SLAP TO RONALD SO THAT HE STOPS SHOUTING. SHUT UP YOU BOTH. THIS IS NOT THE TIME TO FIGHT. I DON'T KNOW THAT JAMES HAVE MAGICAL POWERS OR NOT. WE EVEN DON'T KNOW WHO HAS DONE THIS? I KNOW. JAMES TOLD THEM THE WHOLE STORY. EVERYTHING. EVERY ONE BELIEVED HIM EVEN RONALD. BUT YOU ARE NOT AS POWERFUL AS SATEN. 'I WILL EXPLAIN HIM' SAID CHRIS.

SEE WE WILL DIE. EITHER IF YOU ARE WITH SATEN OR WITH US YOU WILL DIE. WHY SATEN WILL TAKE NON- MAGIC PEOPLE. HE WILL KILL YOU. IT IS BETTER THAT YOU DO GOOD DEEDS BEFORE DYING. RONALD UNDERSTOOD EVERYTHING AND HE CAME TO HELP THEM.

THE PLAN IS ABOUT THAT WE WOULD FIRST FIND OUT HOW SATEN WOULD DIE. WE WOULD FIND OUT THIS BY ENTERING HIS PALACE. WE WOULD KILL THE PERSON WHOM SATEN TRUST THE MOST AND THEN

WE WOULD TAKE THEIR COSTUME AND WE WOULD MAKE OUR FACE SAME TO SAME THEN WE WOULD ENTER HIS CABIN AND SOMEHOW WE WOULD ASK HIM ABOUT HIS PAST; WE WOULD SOMEHOW GET TO KNOW THAT HOW HE WOULD DIE; WE WOULD DO THIS. WE WOULD ALSO ASK HIM THAT HOW WE CAN GO BACK IN TIME AND THEN WE WOULD GO AND IT WOULD BE RIGHT AGAIN. BEFORE WE START KILLING SATEN WE HAVE TO FIRST SOMEHOW DEFEAT HIS 100 DEATHLY SPIRITS AND FOR THAT ALSO I HAVE A PLAN. THE PLAN IS THAT WE WOULD ASK SATEN WHERE THE DEATHLY SPIRITS ARE; WE WOULD FIX VERY MUCH MACHINE GUNS AND FIRE AND WE WOULD FIRST PUT FIRE AND THEN WE WOULD START SHOOTING AND IF NOTHING HAPPENS, WE WOULD ASK SATEN ABOUT IT. SO WE WOULD START THIS PLAN ON 10 APRIL. THEY WENT TO SLEEP. JAMES ASKED THEM TO COME WITH HIM AND SLEEP SO THAT NO ONE DIE.

On the other side no one tried to overcome Saten. He went in an open area and over there were many people and the camera man. There were more than 10000 people. Saten shouted 'now I am the king, you have to follow my orders and if someone tries not to follow my orders and he tries to kill me, you all know what will happen, he would die, I want to tell you that now you will have to put your faith in me.' James Cook has escaped from the prison and if someone tries to help him also, he

WOULD DIE AND IF SOMEONE KNOWS THAT WHERE IS HENRY, HE WOULD ALSO DIE. THE PEOPLE WHO WANT TO COME WITH ME COME IN FRONT AND IF SOMEONE DON'T DO LIKE THIS, THE RESULT WOULD BE DEATH.

HE LAUGHED. HE SAID WHY SO MUCH OF SILENCE IS THERE; YOU DON'T HAVE THINK A LOT JUST COME WITH ME OR DIE.

A MAN CAME AND THE OTHER AND MANY MORE CAME THEN THEY STOPPED COMING. A MAN CAME IN FRONT AND SAID, 'DYING JUST NOW IS BETTER THAT WE DO WORK WITH YOU AND I AM NOT AFRAID OF DEATH.' EVERYONE LEFT STARTED SUPPORTING THAT MAN. SATEN SAID, 'YOU WOULD DIE. EVERYONE WOULD DIE, UGOLOVINERIOVOSA.' THE PEOPLE LEFT WERE DEAD. HE SAID, 'THIS ONLY SHOULD HAPPEN WITH THEM.' HE WENT TO THE REPORTERS AND HE KILLED THEM. HE GAVE THE C.D WHICH THEY MADE TO ONE OF HIS FORCE MEMBER. SATEN VANISHED FROM THERE. HE WENT TO ANOTHER COUNTRY AND OVER THERE ALSO HE DID LIKE THIS ONLY AND PEOPLE WERE MUCH AFRAID OF HIM AFTER SEEING THE VIDEO

ON TV SO FIRST TIME ONLY EVERY ONE
CAME AND HE HAD ALMOST CONQUERED
HALF OF THE EARTH; HE SAID, 'TODAY
MUCH WORK IS DONE AND TOMORROW WE
WOULD DESTROY EARTH.'

AND THEN JAMES WOKE UP. HE MADE
THE OTHERS ALSO WAKE AND HE TOLD
THEM THAT THEY SHOULD NOT SLEEP,
THEY SHOULD START THEIR WORK JUST
NOW ONLY. HE OPENED THE T.V AND THEY
SAW THE NEWS; THEY WERE VERY SAD
TO SEE IT. WE SHOULD START WITH OUR
WORK.

WE HAVE TO FIRST GET THE MAP OF
THE PALACE. WITHOUT IT WE WOULD
NOT BE ABLE TO ATTACK AND IF WE
ASK SOMEONE THEY WOULD NOT TELL US
BECAUSE THE PEOPLE IN THE PALACE
ARE VERY BAD, THEY WOULD SAY YOU
DON'T KNOW. FOR THIS I HAVE A PLAN. THE
MAP IS KEPT WITH HIM M.R OCKWILL WHO
IS MY BEST FRIEND, USE TO WORK IN THE
PALACE AND HE WAS AT THE HIGHEST
POST AFTER THE KING. THE KING HAD

GIVEN HIM THE PHOTOCOPY OF THE MAP TO KEEP SAFELY AND I AM GOING TO HIS HOUSE TO GET IT.

JAMES TOOK THE PLANE AND WENT TO AMERICA. AFTER AN HOUR HE REACHED AMERICA. WHOLE AMERICA WAS BURNED. NOTHING WAS LEFT. THERE WERE DEAD BODIES EVERYWHERE.

JAMES FELT VERY BAD. HE WAS WALKED FOR A LONG TIME TO FIND A CAR. WHEN HE WAS NEAR A BRIDGE, HE FOUND AN OLD B.M.W. THE KEY WAS THERE IN THE CAR, BUT IT WAS INSIDE THE CAR BUT THE CAR WAS LOCKED.

JAMES TOOK A BRICK AND BANGED IT WITH THE WINDOW. THE WINDOW TURNED INTO ASHES. HE TOOK THE KEY, OPENED THE GATE AND WENT TO M.R OCKWILL'S HOUSE.

HIS HOUSE WAS BURNED. THE DOOR WAS LYING ON THE ROAD. THE TERIST HAD FALLEN INSIDE THE HOUSE BUT THERE WAS SOME SPACE TO GO IN. JAMES ENTERED THE HOUSE A SOFA AND A TABLE WERE JUST SEEN AS EVERYTHING WAS DESTROYED. JAMES FELT AS BAD

AS A PERSON FELLS WHEN HE IS GOING TO
PRISON. HE WENT A LITTLE FARTHER AND
HE STOOPED. HE SAW A LETTER. JAMES
PICKED IT UP. SOMEONE HAS SCRIBBLED
IN IT. IT SAID THAT I KNOW THAT WHY
HAVE YOU COME HERE. YOU ARE HERE
FOR THE MAP. THE HEADMASTER OF
REDSCOUT HAD SENT ME. I KNEW THAT
YOU WILL NEED THE MAP. THE KING DIDN'T
GIVE ME, I STOLE IT. I AM SORRY TO TELL
LIE BUT I HAD TO DO THAT. THIS LETTER
IS THERE TO TELL YOU THE LOCATIONS.
I KNOW THAT YOU HAVE GOT LOADS OF
AMMO NATION AS THE CAR WAS KEPT
BY ME. I THINK YOU WILL NEED MORE
ARMOR. FOR THAT A TRUNK IS WAITING
FOR YOU. THE MAP IS IN THE TRUNK BUT
YOU HAVE TO FIND IT. THE TRUNKS ARE
KEPT BEHIND THE SOFA. ALL THIS YOUR
FATHER AND PROFESSOR DAIFOIO HAS
TOLD ME TO DO. NO ONE KNOWS THAT YOU
ARE ON EARTH, LEAVING YOUR PARENTS
AND PROFESSOR DAIFOIO. MEET YOU IN
REDSCOUT.

ALL THE BEST!

WITH BEST REGARDS FROM MR. OCKWILL

JAMES WENT TOWARDS THE SOFA. 5 TRUNKS WERE LYING. IT WAS SEALED WITH LEATHER. THE TOP PORTION OF A CHEST WAS BURNED AND A BIG HOLE APPEARED. HE PUT HIS HAND IN THE CHEST AND FOUND THAT ONE LETTER WAS THERE. HE WENT TOWARDS THE TABLE WHICH WAS BESIDE THAT SOFA. HE PICKED IT UP AND THREW IT ON THE GROUND. CRASH! AND THE FOUR LEG OF THE CHAIR BROKE. 2 LEGS HAD BEEN BROKEN INTO PIECES. JAMES PICKED THE FIRST LEG AND BANGED IT ON THE CHEST. THERE WAS AGAIN A BIG HOLE. HE KEPT N DOING THIS. AFTER SOMETIME, THE CHEST HAD BROKEN INTO 3 HALF'S. JAMES PICKED UP THE LETTER AND READ IT LOUDLY.

I AM OCKWILL. THIS LETTER IS THERE TO TELL YOU THAT, THERE IS ONE CORD AND A BROKEL BOOK IN THIS CHEST. THE MAP IS ALSO HERE.

BY THERE WAS A WOOD LYING ON THE CHEST. IT WAS SHINY BROWN WITH

DIAMONDS ATTACHED IN IT. JAMES PICKED IT UP AND STARTED EXAMINING IT. THERE WAS A PAPER COMING OUT. IT SAID 'FRIOTU'. SOMETHING WAS WRITTEN DOWN ON IT. IT SAID THAT IT BREAKS WOOD.

HE KEPT THE CORD ON THE SOFA AND STARTED TOUCHING THE TRUNK. HE FELT THAT SOMETHING WAS INSIDE THE TRUNK. HE TOOK A KNIFE AND CUT THE TRUNK. HE FOUND AN OLD PAPER. IT WAS HAVING YELLOW SPOTS. IT WAS THE MAP. IT WAS VERY BIG. JAMES DELIGHTED TO SEE IT.

HE KEPT THE MAP AND STARTED OPENING THE OTHER TRUNKS. HE TRIED FOR HOURS BUT IT DIDN'T OPENED. JAMES SAT DOWN EXHAUSTED AND STARTED THINKING FOR AN IDEA TO OPEN THE TRUNK. THEN HE REMEMBERED THAT BROKEL CAN DO IT. HE RUSHED TO THE SOFA AND STARTED EXAMINE THE PAPER.

HE PICKED UP THE CORD AND SAID FRIOTU. THERE WAS A BANG AND THE TRUNKS HAD TURNED INTO ASHES.

THERE WERE 100S OF MACHINEGUN, HANDGUNS, SHOTGUN AND 200 BOW AND ARROW. JAMES PICKED UP THE TRUNKS AND KEPT IT IN THE PLANE. HE TOOK THE CORD AND KEPT IT N THE SEAT OF THE DRIVER. HE TOOK A PHOTO OF M.R OCKWILL AND SAT ON THE DRIVER SEAT. CREAK! (A SOUND LIKE SOMETHING HAS BROKEN). JAMES STOOD UP TO SEE AND HE SAW THAT HIS CORD HAS BROKEN. HE TRIED TO PUT SALOTAPE AND USE IT BUT IT WAS USELESS. HE THREW THE CORD AND WENT TO SLEEP.

THE NEXT MORNING HE WOKE UP. HE TOOK OUT THE MAP AND SPREAD IT ON THE TABLE.

HERE IS THE PLACE WHERE SATEN SIT AND NEAR IT ONLY IS A PLACE WHERE HE SLEEPS. WE HAD TO GO THIS WAY. FOR THE STARTING OF THE PLAN SOMEONE HAD TO GO FIRST IN THE PALACE AND THAT MAN WOULD FIND OUT THE PEOPLE OF WHOM SATEN IS FOND OF.

THE PERSON WOULD BE WATSON AND I HAVE A GADGET FOR ALL OF YOU AND IT IS A GUN. IT IS NOT AN ORDINARY GUN

BUT IN THIS GUN YOU HAD NOT TO PUT
BULLETS. IT MAKES BULLETS ON ITS OWN
AND YOU CAN SHOOT 1000 OF BULLETS
WITHOUT RELOADING. WATSON, TAKE
IT AND GO IN THE PALACE, TAKE THE
MAP ALSO AND TOMORROW GIVE US THE
NAME OF PEOPLE. THIS IS THE CAMERA
WHICH I AM PUTTING SO THAT WE GET TO
KNOW WHAT ARE YOU DOING AND STEAL
A CORD FOR THAT, I WOULD TRY TO DO A
BROKEL AND IN ANY DANGER WEAR THIS
WATCH AND IF YOU WANT A HELP THEM
PRESS THIS RED BUTTON AND NOW YOU
GO. THEY ALL SAT DOWN AND STARTED
WATCHING HIM. WATSON I WOULD TELL
YOU WHAT TO DO EVERYWHERE AND
PLEASE YOU DON'T APPLY YOUR BRAIN.
IN YOUR GUN ONE BUTTON IS THERE, IF
YOU PRESS IT THEN TO BUTTONS MORE
WOULD COME AND IN THAT ONE WOULD
BE FOR FAINTING AND ONE FOR KILLING.
THERE IS A PROBLEM IN THE GUN AND IT
IS THAT THE LOCK SYSTEM COMES DOWN
MINES IF YOU DON'T WANT TO LOCK IT
THEN TOO IT WOULD BE LOCKED BECAUSE
THE BUTTON IS VERY LOOSE AND IF I SAY

TO LOAD IT THEN DON'T SAY WHAT IS IT. JAMES GAVE HIM A PAPER ON WHICH DIALOGUES WERE WRITTEN. NOW GO THESE ARE YOUR. IN THIS PAPER, IT IS WRITTEN WHAT TO SPEAK WHERE. WHEN YOU WOULD COME NEAR THE PALACE YOU WOULD FIND TWO GUARDS. TELL THEM THAT YOUR NAME IS DAVID HOSBERG AND YOU HAVE COME TO BE WITH LORD SATEN. AFTER THAT WHATEVER I WOULD SAY YOU DO IT. WATSON WENT; THEY SAT DOWN TO WATCH HIM. WATSON REACHED THE DOOR OF THE PALACE.

TWO GUARDS STOOD THERE. THEY WERE HOLDING TWO SWORDS.

AS JAMES REACHED THERE, THEY CLOSED THEIR SWORD TO BLOCK THE WAY.

WHO ARE YOU AND WHY YOU HAVE COME?

MY NAME IS DAVID HOSBERG AND I AM HERE TO BE WITH LORD SATEN.

GO INSIDE. WATSON WENT INSIDE.

JAMES KEPT ON GUIDING HIM. A MAN CAME IN FRONT OF WATSON.

'WATSON, ASK HIM THE DEAREST PERSON OF SATEN.' JAMES SAID.

HEY, YOUNG MAN CAN YOU TELL ME THE MOST DEAR PEOPLE OF SATEN.

OH! YOU DON'T KNOW. I DOUBT THAT YOU ARE A SPY OF THAT MAN, HENRY.

HE WENT FROM THERE. WATSON STARTED TO MOVE. WHEN WATSON WAS NEAR A CABIN, JAMES ORDERED HIM TO HIDE BY A SHELF.

WATSON, RELOAD YOUR GUN AND ON THE FAINTER SYSTEM.

A MAN PASSED BY WATSON.

WATSON, COME OUT OF THE SHELF AND SAY EXACTLY THIS.

HEY, TELL ME THE DEAREST PEOPLE OF SATEN OR I WILL KILL YOU. AND YOU POINT YOUR GUN TOWARDS HIM.

WATSON DID EXACTLY LIKE THIS. WHEN HIS SENTENCE AS OVER, THAT PERSON TOOK OUT HIS GUN.

WATSON GO AWAY AND HIDE BY THE WALL. WATSON DID BACK FLIP AND HID BY THE WALL.

NOW, WATSON WHATEVER I WILL SAY, YOU DO IT. RUN AND SHOOT THAT MAN, AFTER SHOOTING YOU DO FRONT FLIP.

WATSON RAN AND SHOT HIM, HE DID THEN FRONT FLIP.

JUST BECAUSE OF THE FLIP, WATSON WAS SAVED BECAUSE THAT MAN ALSO SHOT AT THAT MOMENT.

WATSON, NOW YOU SOMEHOW MANAGE A ROPE. YOU TIE HIM WITH IT.

THEN GO IN THE CABIN, THERE WILL BE A BALCONY.

THROW HIM FROM IT. MY CAR WOULD BE STANDING THERE.

WATSON'S LUCK WAS VERY NICE. AT THAT MOMENT A PERSON PASSED WITH A ROPE.

WATSON FAINT THAT PERSON. HE TIED THEM WITH ROPES.

HE TOOK THEM IN THE CABIN. HE TOOK OUT HIS GUN.

AS HE STEPPED, SOMEONE STARTED SHOOTING.

WATSON SAT DOWN AND STARTED FINDING THAT PERSON.

A PERSON WITH BLACK SUIT, BLACK GLASSES, BLACK SHOES STOOD NEAR THE BALCONY.

HE LOOKED EXACTLY LIKE MEN IN BLACK. THEY WERE CONTINUOUSLY SHOOTING EACH OTHER.

THAT PERSON'S BULLETS WERE OVER. HE THREW HIS GUN AND JUMPED ON WATSON.

HE SNATCHED HIS GUN AND THREW IT.

HE GAVE A PUNCH ON WATSON'S STOMACH. THEN HE GAVE ON HIS FACE.

HE HELD HIS HAND AND KICKED ON HIS HANDS.

WATSON, CAN YOU HEAR ME? I AM CHRIS. JAMES IS NOT THERE. I WILL GUIDE YOU.

TAKE THE TWO PEOPLE NEAR THE BALCONY. THROW THEM AND THEN YOU ALSO JUMP.

NOTHING WILL HAPPEN BECAUSE JAMES IS THERE.

HE WILL HANDLE THE SITUATION. WATSON WAS NOT SURE WHAT HE WAS GOING TO DO.

HE KICKED THAT MAN WITH HIS WHOLE MIGHT ON HIS MAIN POINT.

THAT MAN ROARED WITH PAIN. WATSON PICKED THEM AND THREW THEM FROM THE BALCONY.

JAMES WAS THERE. THAT MAN HAD GOT UP. HE WAS HOLDING WATSON'S GUN.

WATSON QUICKLY STOOD ON THE BALCONY AND JUMPED.

AS WATSON FELL, THAT MAN SHOT HIM. TWO BULLETS DIRECTLY HIT WATSON'S CHEST.

JAMES TOOK OUT HIS GUN AND SHOT THAT MAN. HE THREW A ROPE AND STARTED CLIMBING ON IT.

HE REACHED THE BALCONY. HE TOOK THAT MAN AND THREW HIM ON THE CAR.

HE TOOK WATSON AND PUT HIM ON THE BACK SEAT AND WENT TO HIS LAB.

HI, EVERYONE I AM BACK. TAKE WATSON TO THE HOSPITAL.

NOW LISTEN ME CAREFULLY, CLOSE THE DOOR AND BRING THE FIRST PERSON AND THE OTHER TWO YOU SOMEWHERE HIDE.

NO ONE WOULD OPEN THE DOOR TILL THE TIME I SAY. OK. NOW GO. SO WHAT'S YOUR NAME?

I ASKED YOU WHAT YOUR NAME IS! MY NAME IS STEVE KREA. YOU KNOW WHAT'S MY NAME?

NO I DON'T KNOW. MY NAME IS JAMES COOK. YOUR NAME IS JAMES COOK, I WILL NOT LEAVE YOU, YOU ARE THE ENEMIES OF MASTER. STEAVE HELD HIS NECK AND STARTED PRESSING IT.

LEAVE ME LEAVE ME. YOU ...

JAMES BEAT HIM WITH HIS LEG ON HIS STOMACH. SIT OVER THERE ONLY OR YOU WOULD BE KILLED. STEAVE RAN TOWARDS A KNIFE.

HE HELD IT AND RAN TO KILL HENRY. JAMES HELD HIS HAND AND SLAPPED HIM.

HE FELL ON THE FLOOR. JAMES TOOK OUT HIS GUN. SIT DOWN ON THE CHAIR OR I WILL KILL YOU.

TELL ME THE PEOPLE WHOM SATEN LIKE THE MOST. MASTER HAS SAID NOT TO TELL ANYONE ABOUT THE PALACE.

TELL ME OR I KILL WILL YOU. YOU KILL ME BUT I WILL NOT TELL. I KNOW THE

OTHER WAY ALSO TO ASK THE TRUTH. GET UP! I SAID GET UP.

JAMES HELD HIS CALLER AND THREW HIM ON THE FLOOR. HERE IS A WOOD FOR YOU.

HE PICKED IT UP AND STARED BEATING HIM. TAKE THE FIRST. AUUUUAAAAA! LEAVE ME. TAKE THE SECOND! AEEEUU! TAKE THE THIRD. YOU DO ANYTHING I WILL NOT TELL YOU.

TAKE THE THIRD FOURTH, FIFTH, SIXTH, SEVENTH, AND THEN HE BEAT HIM ON HIS HAND; ON HIS MOUTH; ON HIS FACE; ON HIS LEG; ON HIS BACK; ON HIS NECK; ON HIS STOMACH.

HE WAS BADLY INJURED. JAMES BEAT HIM WITH HIS LEG THREE TIMES. HE PICKED HIM UP AND THREW HIM.

HE BANGED WITH THE WALL. HE FELL ON THE FLOOR AND WENT UNCONSCIOUS.

JAMES WENT OUTSIDE THE ROOM AND CALLED CHRIS. CHRIS I NEED YOUR HELP. THE PLAN IS THIS THAT THE MAN STEVE IS NOT OPENING HIS MOUTH.

SO I HAVE A PLAN. WHEN I WAS BEATING HIM, I ASKED HIM THAT WHO

ARE THE PEOPLE WHOM HE CAN GIVE HIS LIFE FOR.

AND THEY ARE HIS CHILDREN AND HIS WIFE. AND I WANT YOU TO BRING THEM HERE.

YOU WOULD TELL THEM THE WHOLE STORY AND IF THEY CORPORATE THEN OUR PLAN IS THAT WE WOULD TAKE A FAKE GUN AND WE WOULD PUT RED SAUCE IN THEIR BODY; IT WOULD LOOK LIKE THAT WE HAVE REALLY SHOT THEM AND THEN STEVE CAN OPEN HIS MOUTH AND IF THEY DON'T CORPORATE SEND THEM BACK.

I WOULD BEAT HIM A LOT AND IF HE OPENS HIS MOUTH I WILL TAKE HIS MEMORY OUT BY MY MEMORY TAKER.

NOW GO AND I AM MAKING HIM COME CONSCIOUS. JAMES WENT TO THE ROOM BACK.

HEY YOU GET UP. JAMES BEAT HIM WITH HIS LEG AND HE DROPPED SOME WATER ON HIM, HE BECAME CONSCIOUS.

I AM ASKING YOU LAST TIME TELL ME OR I APPLY MY LAST WAY. JAMES GOT A CALL FROM SOMEONE.

IT WAS OF CHRIS. HELLO CHRIS! JAMES I CALLED YOU TO TELL THAT THEY WOULD HELP US AND I AM OUTSIDE THE ROOM AND IF YOU SAY THEN I BRING THEM.

CHRIS ITS BRILLIANT OF YOU. JUST WAIT FOR A MINUTE AND THEN YOU COME. APPROXIMATELY 1 MINUTE ONLY. BY.

STEVE YOU TELL ME OR SOMETHING VERY BAD IS GOING TO HAPPEN WITH YOU. JAMES PUT HIS GUN ON HIS HEAD; CHRIS CAME WITH A LADY AND TWO CHILDREN. BESSIE, REAN AMELIA WHY YOU HAVE COME HERE? WHO HAS CALLED YOU.

SHEAVE LOOKED ANGRILY TOWARDS HENRY. YOU I WILL KILL YOU. IT'S OUR MATTER, WHY YOU HAD CALLED MY FAMILY.

IF YOU DON'T TELL ME THEN I WOULD KILL THEM. YOU CAN'T DO THIS. I WOULD DO THIS IF YOU DON'T TELL ME.

CHRIS PUT THE GUN ON HIS WIFE. FIRST NUMBER WILL BE OF YOUR WIFE. NOOOOOOOO! YES OF COURSE WE WILL DO IT.

I AM COUNTING TILL 1.....2.....3 AND THE LAST 3 KILL HER. NO BESSIE YOU CAN'T LEAVE ME.

YOU ARE SO BAD. WHATEVER BAD WORDS SAID TO YOU WOULD BE LESS, YOU ARE SO BAD. HE PICKED UP A GUN.

AS HE WAS GOING TO PRESS THE TRIGGER CHRIS CONTROLLED THE SITUATION. HEY MISTER IF YOU PRESS THE TRIGGER IT WOULD BE YOUR CHILD.

SIT ON THE CHAIR, LEAVE THE GUN AND TELL US. HE SAT ON THE CHAIR AND HE GAVE THE GUN TO HENRY.

MAX DESOREOS, JOE POCKIROS, WAYNE DAVE, LEONONEL SART, GEOFEST MACROX. OK! NOW YOU CAN GO.

CHRIS TAKE HIS MEMORY. CHRIS TOOK HIS MEMORY AND HE WENT. JAMES WENT TO THE OTHERS AND THEY ALSO SAID THESE NAMES ONLY AND THEY ALL WENT.

JAMES CALLED A MEETING. NOW WE KNOW THE NAMES OF PEOPLE AND WE HAVE TO KILL THEM AND AFTER THAT YOU KNOW.

IN THIS MISSION I WOULD GO AND I DON'T WANT ANY HELP IF I WOULD BE NEEDING A HELP THEN I WOULD CALL YOU.

WATSON I TOLD YOU TO BRING A CORD, HAD YOU BROUGHT IT. NO HENRY. SO I HAVE TO GET A CORD ALSO FOR ME. I AM LEAVING.

HE TOOK HIS FAINTER AND MEMORY GUN. WHEN HE CAME TOWARDS THE DOOR, HE WORE A MASK SO THAT HE COULD NOT BE SEEN.

JAMES SAW SOMETHING IRREGULAR WAS WRITTEN ON THE MAIN DOOR. HE TOOK A PHOTO OF IT AND WENT FURTHER.

THE DOORMAN LOOKED TO HIM A CRUEL MAN. YOU MAN, WHY YOU HAVE COME HERE, GET AWAY FROM HERE AND SHOW YOUR FACE. HE TOOK OUT HIS MEMORY GUN AND HE TOOK THE MEMORY OF BOTH THE DOORMEN AND HE CAME INSIDE. HE THOUGHT TO START WITH MAX. WHEN HE CAME BETWEEN THE CASTLES, HE FOUND A MAN.

JAMES THOUGHT PUT THE GUN ON HIS FACE AND THEN BLACKMAIL HIM TO TELL AND THEN I WOULD TAKE OUT HIS

MEMORY. HEY! MAN TELL ME THE WAY TO THE CABIN OF MAX.

WHY? YOU DON'T KNOW? TELL ME WHERE IT IS OR I WOULD SHOOT YOU. OK I AM TELLING.

GO FROM HERE LEFT THEN RIGHT AND GO A LITTLE FAR AND THERE IS MAX'S CABIN.

JAMES TOOK HIS MEMORY AND TO GO TO MAX'S CABIN. WHEN HE REACHED HIS CABIN HE FOUND TWO DOORMEN. HE TOOK THEIR MEMORY AND WENT INSIDE.

HELLO M.R DESOREOS. WHO ARE YOU AND WHO ALLOWED YOU TO COME INSIDE?

SECURITY SECURITY. NO ONE WOULD COME.. I HAVE TAKEN THEIR MEMORY AND JUST KNOW THEY ARE UNCONSCIOUS. THEY WILL SOON BECOME CONSCIOUS BUT TILL THAT TIME YOU WOULD NOT BE HERE..

JAMES TOOK OUT HIS FAINTER AND HE FAINTED HIM, HE SAW THAT THE BALCONY WAS ATTACHED TO HIS CABIN. 1GUARD WAS STANDING THERE ONLY.

THERE WAS A WINDOW WITH NO MIRROR SO HE SHOT THAT GUARD WITH HIS FAINTER AND HE CAME IN THE BALCONY.

HIS TRUCK WAS NOT PRESENT THERE. I KNEW THAT THIS PROBLEM CAN OCCUR SO THAT IS WHY I BROUGHT THIS GADGET.

IT WAS A MAP AND AT THE END THERE WAS A MACHINE. IT WAS NEITHER VERY BIG NOR VERY SMALL.

IT WAS COVERED WITH ALPHABETS EVERYWHERE. ON THAT YOU HAD TO TYPE THE THINGS NAME YOU WANT TO COME. HE TYPED HIS TRUCK'S NAME AND THEN ITS NUMBER THEN ITS LOCATION AND THEN THE LOCATION WHERE HE WANT IT TO COME AND IN TWO MINUTE THAT CAR CAME.

JAMES THREW MAX ON THE TRUCK. HIS CAR HAD A SPECIAL FEATURE AND THAT WAS IF YOU THROW ANYTHING IN HIS TRUCK THEN THE DOOR (WHICH HE HAS PUT ON THE ROOF OF HIS TRUCK SO THAT PEOPLE CANNOT SEE) WOULD OPEN AND IT WOULD CLOSE AGAIN AUTOMATICALLY.

JAMES RUSHED TO GO TOWARDS JOE. ON THE WAY JAMES FOUND A SWEEPER.

HE WAS ONCE HIS SERVANT AND HIS
NAME WAS KANE HILLARY. HE DIDN'T
WANT TO TALK TO HIM BUT HE THOUGHT
TO ASK HIM WHERE WAS JOE'S OFFICE.

HEY KANE, REMEMBER ME! HENRY,
YES I REMEMBER YOU! CAN I BE OF ANY
HELP? YES, IF YOU WANT TO HELP. WHICH
HELP? I WANT TO KNOW WHERE THE
CABIN OF JOE IS.?

HENRY, JUST TURN BACK AND THE
ROOM IN THE FRONT, GO IN IT AND THEN
THERE WOULD BE A SMALL GLOBE AND
YOU ROTATE IT AND THEN SATEN'S ROOM
WOULD COME THEN JOE AND IF YOU GO A
LITTLE FAR THEN NEAR THAT ONLY ALL
THE FOUR MOST LIKED PEOPLE BY SATEN
ARE THERE JUST LEAVING ONE AND IF
YOU WANT TO KNOW THE ROOM OF OTHER
I CAN TELL.

NO, THANKS A LOT KANE. AND BE
AWARE OF THEM, THEY KNOW MAGIC
AND SOMETIME SATEN SAYS THAT THEY
ARE HIS FRIENDS AND THEY ARE FROM
REDSCOUTER COUNTRY.

BUT I IMAGINE WHICH COUNTRY'S NAME
IS REDSCOUT AND WHICH UNIVERSITY'S

NAME IS REDSCOUT. AFTER HEARING THIS HE FIRST THOUGHT THAT HE HAD FEAR OF NOTHING BUT NOW HE GOT TO KNOW THE TRUTH. HE HAD FEAR FROM FEAR.

'I ALSO DON'T KNOW KANE.' SAID JAMES HASTILY. HE WENT IN THAT ROOM. IT WAS A VERY LARGE ROOM WITH UNCOUNTABLE THINGS. HE WAS NOT ABLE TO FIND THE GLOBE. JAMES LIED ON THE BED.

AFTER A MINUTE HE FOUND A DIAMOND. JAMES HELD IT AND AS HE HELD IT THE BED BROKE.

JAMES CAME DOWN IN AN UNKNOWN PLACE. IT WAS DARK EVERYWHERE. HE WAS NOT ABLE TO SEE ANYTHING.

HE SAW SOME SWITCHES AND WHEN HE PRESSED THEM, THE LIGHT CAME BUT AFTER SOMETIME IT WENT.

WHO IS THERE? COME FORWARD, DON'T HIDE. JAMES SAW HUNDREDTHS OF ZOMBIES WERE HEADING TOWARDS HIM.

HE TOOK OUT HIS GUN AND SHOT 10 OF THEM. THEN THEY JUMPED TOWARDS AND HE TURNED TO RUN BUT HE COULDN'T ESCAPE BECAUSE THERE WAS A WALL.

JAMES THOUGHT TO FIGHT. WHEN THE FIRST ZOMBIE CAME HE TOOK OUT HIS GUN AND SHOT ON HIS FACE THEN FROM THERE THE SECOND ONE CAME, THEN THIRD THEN FOURTH, THEN FIFTH AND THEN THE NUMBER WENT TO 10. JAMES HELD ON ZOMBIE'S SHOULDER AND FLEW INTO THE AIR.

WHILE HE WAS IN THE AIR, HE BEAT ALL THE ZOMBIES.

HE FELL ON THE GROUND. EVERY ZOMBIE WAS NEAR HIM. JAMES JUMPED IN THE AIR.

HE FELL ON THE ZOMBIES HEAD. IT WAS A NICE OPPORTUNITY.

HE TOOK OUT HIS GUN AND SHOT ALL OF THEM. EVERY ONE FELL ON THE GROUND.

JAMES WAS EXHAUSTED. HE WAS BREATHING LOUDLY. HE SAT ON THE FLOOR.

HE LEANED HIS HEAD NEAR THE WALL. HE HAD JUST FALLEN ASLEEP WHEN A NEW ROUND OF ZOMBIES CAME.

A ZOMBIE PICKED HIM UP AND THREW HIM. HE WAS CATCHED BY THE OTHER ZOMBIE.

THE ZOMBIES WERE PLAYING CATCH AND CATCH. THE GAME WAS THAT IF THEY MISS A CHANCE, JAMES WILL BE BEAT BY HUNTERS.

JAMES WAS TILL NOW BEAT 5 TIMES. JAMES WAS NOT ABLE TO SEE ANYTHING.

THE PICTURE IN HIS RETINA WAS GETTING FAINTER. HE WAS GOING HERE AND THERE.

AFTER A LONG TIME THE GAME WAS END AND HENRY'S HEALTH WAS GETTING WORST.

HE WAS ROAMING HERE AND THERE AND FINALLY HE FELL. HE WAS ABLE TO SEE SOMETHING.

A MAN WITH TWO SWORDS WAS COMING. HE WAS HOLDING A HANDCUFF.

HE PUT IT ON HENRY'S HAND AND PUT HIM IN A PRISON.

IT WAS VERY SMALL PRISON. HE THREW HIM OVER THERE AND SAID THAT HE WOULD START ASKING HIM AFTER 1 HOUR.

JAMES TURNED HIS FACE AND SAW A LINE. HE GOT TO KNOW THAT

IT IS A SECRET ROOM. SO HE STARTED SEARCHING THINGS TO OPEN IT.

JAMES NOTICED TOWARDS THE GROUND. AT THE EDGE, THERE WAS A COIN OF 2 MILLIMETER STUCK IN THE GROUND.

HE TOUCHED IT AND THE LINE TURNED INTO AN OPEN DOOR. HE FOUND A MAN HANGED WITH A WALL. HE WAS LOOKING LIKE HE WAS DEAD BUT HE WAS NOT.

JAMES OPENED THE NEXT DOOR. HE KEPT ON OPENING BUT EVERY TIME THERE WAS THE SAME PICTURE..

WHEN HE REACHED THE TENTH (IT WAS THE LAST) OVER THERE WAS A MAN BUT HE WAS NOT DEAD. HE SET HIM FREE. THEY SAT DOWN TO TALK.

WHAT IS HAPPENING AND WHAT IS YOUR NAME? SEE WHAT HAPPENED THAT LIKE YOU ONLY WE ALSO CAME TO DEFEAT SATEN BUT WE WERE CAUGHT.

THEY WOULD BEAT US TILL THE TIME WE DON'T TELL THEM THE WHOLE STORY AND THIS WOULD LEAD TO DEATH.

MY NAME IS MICHEL CHRF DON'T WORRY I WOULD DO ALL THE THINGS RIGHT. IT

IS IMPOSSIBLE. NO, I HAVE AN IDEA. OUR PLAN IS THIS THAT I HAVE A GUN.

AS I KNOW THAT THE 8 PEOPLE ARE NOT DEAD. YOU HAVE TO FREE THEM BECAUSE NOW YOU HAVE ACCESS TO ALL PRISONS.

AFTER SETTING THEM FREE, I WILL BE GIVING YOU FIRST AID AND SOME OTHER THINGS TO CURE THEM.

INCLUDING THE BEST MEDICINES BUT BEFORE, YOU HAVE TO GIVE A LIST OF WHICH TYPES OF THINGS YOU NEED.

I WILL PROVIDE IT ALL TO YOU. IT IS MY HEADACHE THAT HOW I WILL PROVIDE.

APPROXIMATELY AFTER 50MIN I WILL BE WAITING FOR YOU ALL IN MY PRISON. AFTER THAT I WILL HANDLE.

MICHAEL GAVE A BIG LIST WHICH INCLUDED THESE THINGS.

#1) COTTON
#2) ANTISEPTIC LOTIONS
#3) FLEXON, ACILOCK AND LUPIHEM (MEDICINES)
#4) BANDAGE AND KNEE CAP
#5) WATER

#6) ENERGY DRINKS

#7) FOOD

#8) GLUCOSE

#9) IRON TABLETS AND VITAMIN TABLETS

#10) JUICE OF APPLE AND ORANGE

#11) 8 INJECTION (FOR GETTING RELIEF FROM PAIN.)

JAMES GOT THESE THINGS FROM HIS GADGET. HE GAVE THEM TO MICHAEL.

APPROXIMATELY AFTER 54 MINUTES THEY WERE WITH HENRY. THAT MAN CAME. HE WAS HOLDING A HUNTER AND A CHAIN.

HE DIDN'T SAW THAT ALL THE PRISONERS WERE IN ONE PRISON ONLY.

AS HE CAME, EVERYONE STARTED BEATING HIM AND ACCORDING TO THE PLAN THEY CAME OUT.

NOW YOU ALL SHOULD LEAVE. WON'T YOU COME WITH US. NO I CAN'T, TILL THE TIME I DON'T COMPLETE HIS MISSION I WON'T GO FROM HERE.

JAMES STARTED SEARCHING FOR THE GLOBE. THE ROOM WAS FILLED OF MYSTERIOUS THINGS.

THERE WAS A STATUE OF SATEN'S HEAD. JAMES WENT TOWARDS IT.

HE TOUCHED IT AND SOMETHING HAPPENED. THE WALL NEAR IT TURNED INTO A SHELF. THERE WERE DRAWERS IN IT.

HE OPENED IT. NOTHING WAS IN ALL THE DRAWERS BUT SOMETHING WAS THERE IN THE LAST DRAWER.

THERE WAS A CUBIC CUBE. JAMES PICKED IT UP. WHEN HE TOUCHED BOTTOM OF THE CUBE, THE TOP OPENED.

A SMALL STAND CAME OUT. ONE IT WAS A GLOBE. JAMES SNATCHED IT. BUT THAT GLOBE DIDN'T COME OUT.

INSTEAD JAMES GOT AN ELECTRIC SHOCK. JAMES GOT TO KNOW THAT IT IS IMPOSSIBLE.

HE AGAIN WENT TO THE CUBE. SOMETHING WAS WRITTEN DOWN. IT SAID PASSWORD.

A HINT WAS ALSO WRITTEN. IT SAID THAT THE PASSWORD IS ON THE MAIN GATE.

JAMES REMEMBERED THAT SOMETHING WAS WRITTEN ON THE GATE. JAMES OPENED HIS MOBILE AND WENT TO GALLERY.

A PHOTO WAS THERE ON WHICH IT WAS WRITTEN IN SPANISH MASCULINO. THIS MEANS GLOBE.

JAMES TYPED IT AND THE GLOBE CAME OUT. HE HELD IT AND THE DOOR OPENED.

JAMES WENT INSIDE IT. THERE WERE MANY STAIRS. WHEN JAMES HAD WENT WHOLE DOWN HE FOUND A ROOM.

ON THAT ROOM IT WAS WRITTEN SATEN. HE OPENED IT. A BIG TABLE WAS THERE AND ON THAT A DIARY WAS THERE.

JAMES OPENED IT AND WHAT HE SAW HE WENT MAD. FIRST HE SAW THAT ONE PHOTO WAS THERE AND ON IT CROSS WAS MADE.

DOWN IT WAS WRITTEN WILLIAM ALBUS. JAMES GOT TO KNOW THAT HE IS HIS FATHER.

AFTER IT WAS JAMES COOK'S PHOTO. AFTER IT WAS A PHOTO OF A MAN. DOWN WAS WRITTEN DAIFOI.

UNDER IT WAS A UNIVERSITY. TWO GIGANTIC BOOKS WERE MADE AND ON IT WAS AGAIN A BOOK. AT THE MAIN GATE, IT WAS WRITTEN REDSCOUT.

NOTHING ELSE WAS WRITTEN IN THAT DIARY. AT THE LAST PAGE, THERE WAS A CORD.

JAMES TOOK IT AND WENT TO JOE'S CABIN. HE KILLED JOE AND WENT TO THE OTHER.

IT TOOK 1 HOUR TO KILL EVERYONE. HE SAT IN HIS CAR AND WENT TO THE LAB.

HALF OF THE MISSION IS DONE. NOW THE PEOPLE WHO WANT TO GO FROM THIS GROUP SO GO. I AM SAYING BECAUSE ANYONE WOULD DIE.

SO RAISE YOUR HAND. NO ONE RAISED THEIR HANDS. RONALD CAME IN FRONT. WE ALL ARE NOT AFRAID OF DEATH.

WE WILL BE ALWAYS WITH YOU. EVEN IN THE TIME OF DEATH. IF STONES FALL

FROM THE SKY THEN ALSO WE WILL HOLD YOUR HAND AND COMPLETE OUR MISSION.

WE WILL BE WITH YOU AT EVERY STEP YOU DO. OUR MISSION IS TO HELP YOU FROM OUR HEART AND KILL SATEN.

NO ONE WILL LEAVE YOU. WE WILL BE WITH YOU IN GOOD TIMES AND EVEN IN BAD TIMES.

I THINK I SAID RIGHT MY FRIENDS. EVERYONE CAME IN THE FRONT. YES YOU SAID RIGHT.

A DROP OF TEAR CAME OUT FROM HENRY'S EYES. HE WENT AND HUGGED RONALD. ALL THE OTHER PEOPLE HUGGED HIM.

OK, SO IN MY CAR THERE ARE 5 PEOPLE AND NOW YOU COPY THEIR FACES AND I AM GOING TO PRACTICE BROKEL.

JAMES SAT ON HIS SEAT AND STARTED REMEMBERING THE BROKEL WHICH SATEN SAID.

HE TOOK OUT HIS CORD AND FIRST BROKEL WHICH HE REMEMBERED WAS STRAYED. HE SAID IT AND THERE WAS A BANG AND THE SHELF WHICH WAS IN FRONT OF HIM BROKE.

JAMES REMEMBERED THAT SATEN SAID FRIOTRISM AND THE RESULT WAS THAT THE WOOD LAID FRONT OF HIM WAS CRUCIFIED.

HE REMEMBERED THAT WHEN HE WAS IN THE SHIP, MR. ROLED SAID RIO TRISM HURRICUN. HE TRIED IT AND A BIG HURRICANE CAME.

HE TOOK OUT SOMETHING. IT WAS THE DIARY OF SATEN. HE OPENED IT. JUST ON ONE PAGE ONLY SOME PHOTOS WERE STUCK.

JAMES WAS JUST TURNING THE PAGES RAPIDLY. HE TOOK THE DIARY AND PUT IT ON FIRE. SOME WORDS STARTED APPEARING ON THE DIARY.

THE DIARY FELL ON THE FLOOR AND IT CLOSED. JAMES PICKED IT UP BUT KNOW IT WASN'T OPENING. SOMETHING WAS WRITTEN ON IT.

IT SAID THAT JAMES WAS NOT SATEN SO IT WILL NOT OPEN. JAMES TOOK IT AND BURNED IT.

JAMES WENT OUT. EVERYONE WAS READY. JAMES ALSO GOT READY. WE DO NOT HAVE TO TAKE ANYTHING BECAUSE

THERE WOULD BE A CHECKING. TAKING A CORD IS ALLOWED AND IF SOMETHING HAPPENS THEN YOU CALL ME. WE HAVE TO GO ALONE. BEFORE YOU REACH SATEN'S OFFICE YOU WILL INFORM ME.

I WILL COME AT 4TH NUMBER AND THE FIFTH ONE WILL COME AFTER 10 MINUTES. YOU ALL DON'T HAVE TO COME AT ONE TIME.

THESE ARE YOUR MAPS NOW GO. THEY ALL REACHED. JAMES WAS MAX. CHRIS WAS JOE. RON WAS GEOFEST, JOHN WAS LEONONEL, WATSON WAS WAYNE.

ALL OF THEM REACHED IN SATEN'S OFFICE. THEY ALL SAT DOWN. JAMES STARTED ASKING QUESTIONS

SIR! HOW DID YOU BECOME SO POWERFUL? AND WHY YOU WANT HENRY'S LIFE? I WILL TELL YOU MAX. YOU ALL KNOW ABOUT REDSCOUT AND THE COUNTRY.

YES. SO I WAS ALSO A CHILD IN REDSCOUT AND WAS A NICE BROKELEL. BUT OVER THERE ONE ENEMY OF MINE WAS THERE.

WHOSE NAME IS WILLIAM ALBUS THE FATHER OF JAMES WAS A VERY NICE

BROKELEL PERHAPS THE BEST. HE USED TO OFTEN TEASE ME.

THEN ONE DAY I WENT IN THE RESTRICTED AREA OF LIBRARY. OVER THERE I GOT A BOOK IN THAT A NAME WAS WRITTEN 'THE GOLDEN BALL' AND DOWN IT WAS WRITTEN 'GO TO ANOTHER.

THERE ARE TWO REDSCOUT WHICH IS THE SECOND IS 20¾ DESTROYED. BUT NOW I WILL DESTROY IT WHOLE.

IN THAT REDSCOUT'S LIBRARY I WENT. AGAIN I GOT THAT BOOK AND ON IT WAS WRITTEN "DEFROST FOREST'

SO I WENT IN THAT FOREST. IT WAS NOT A DESCENT FOREST. OVER THERE I GOT A WHOLE BURNED BOOK.

I THOUGHT TO DO IT RIGHT AGAIN BY MY MAGIC. THEN ALSO NOTHING APPEARED SO I TOOK OUT MY LEMON AND DROPPED THE JUICE AND EVERYTHING APPEARED.

IT WAS WRITTEN THAT YOU WILL FIND A ROPE. TAKE IT AND G TO THE LAST TREE. START RUBBING THE TREE. SHE TREE.

START RUBBING THE TREE. TAKE IT IN THE GLASS. PUT I KG OF GOLD AND 100 DIAMONDS.

PUT IT IN THE JUICE AND SLEEP. DON'T WAKE UP TILL THE TIME RAIN DOESN'T FALL.

WHEN RAIN IS STOPPED, YOU WILL FIND A GOLDEN BALL. BESIDE IT WOULD BE A JUICE. IT IS EXTREMELY BAD IN TASTE.

AFTER DRINKING IT, THE BALL WILL BE OPENED. THEN YOU HAVE TO KILL 7 BEST PEOPLE IN BROKEL.

WHENEVER YOU WILL BE IN DANGER THEN THAT 7 SPIRITS WILL COME AND KILL THAT PERSON AND NO ONE CAN DEFEAT THEM.

FOR THAT BALL SAFETY YOU HAVE TO KILL 100 PEOPLE. YOU HAVE TO HIDE THEM. IF SOMEONE TRIES TO TOUCH THAT BALL HE WILL BE KILLED. BECAUSE OF THE 100 PEOPLE.

I DID EXACTLY LIKE THIS. I THOUGHT TO START WITH WILLIAM ALBUS. I WENT IN REDSCOUT. I WAS STANDING FACE TO FACE WITH WILLIAM.

AS I WAS GOING TO KILL HIM THE HEADMASTER OF REDSCOUT CAME. HE SEND ME TO PRISON FOR 9 YEARS.

AFTER COMING OUT FROM PRISON, I KILLED 6 PEOPLE. I WENT STRAIGHT TO WILLIAM. AS I TOUCHED THE GATE, I GOT A SHOCK.

I GOT TO KNOW THAT I CAN'T ENTER REDSCOUT. BUT ONE DAY LUCK ONLY WALKED TOWARDS ME.

THAT PERSON WAS JAMES COOK. I KNEW THAT HE IS VERY POWERFUL SO KNOW I AM BACK OF HIS LIFE BUT THE STORY DOESN'T END HERE.

I STARTED ATTACKING HIM. HE RAN FROM THERE. HE WENT IN THE HEADMASTER'S OFFICE.

THE HEDMASTER SENT HIM ON EARTH. I STARTED PLANING TO COME ON ERTH.. I TRANSFORMED THAT 100 SPIRITS IN MUMMIES AND SENT IT ON EARTH.

EVERYTHING WAS PREPARED. THE MAGE FOR THE ACTUION HALL, LAPESCO AND OTHER PEOPLE WERE ALREADY ON EARTH.

I WAS LOOKING OUT FOR AN OPPORTUNITY. AND I GOT IT. WHEN JAMES WAS SITTING ON THE ROAD BEGGING, I SENT A BALL.

HE TOUCHED IT AND HE LOST HIS MEMORY. HE REMEMBERD THAT HE IS A BIG SCIENTIST. I KEPT ON SENDING IDEAS FOR MAKING NEW GADGETS.

THE PLAN WAS GOING WELL. ACOORIDING TO THE PLAN I AM ON EARTH. SO THIS IS MY PAST.

JAMES GOT UP AND ASKED AGAIN A NEW QUESTION. SIR, HOW CAN THE GOLDEN BALL BE DESTROYED?

I DON'T KNOW NICELY BUT PERHAPES YOU CAN DESTROY THAT BALL THEN WHEN THE OWNER OF THE BALL WILL SAY A VERY STRONG BROKEL POINTING IT TOWARDS HIS GOLDEN BALL.

SIR, HOW CAN WE GO BACK IN TIME. BY CITRUS STONE? IT IS OF REDSCOUT BUT I HAVE STOLEN IT AND IT IS WITH ME. HE HAD HID IT SOMEWHERE. BUT FROM THAT STONE YOU CAN GO BACK IN TIME.

SIR WE WANT TO LOOK THAT BALL. COME TOMORROW. SIR WHERE ARE THOSE

MUMMIES AND HOW WE CAN KILL THEM. THEY ARE IN VOUNTTON PRISON.

YOU CAN KILL THEM BY BULLETS BUT FOR THAT YOU HAVE TO SAY STRAYED ON EVERY GUN FROM WHICH YOU HAVE TO SHOOT THEM.

OK! NOW I THINK WE SHOULD LEAVE.. THEY CAME OUT AND WENT TO THE LAB. WE TOOK A LITTLE REST AND AGAIN JAMES TOLD THEM HIS PLAN.

WE WILL GO AND OVER THERE WILL BE 100 MUMMIES (THEY WERE NOT REPRODUCING THEY WERE JUST FOOLING THEM). WE WILL BE WITH THEM AND AT ANY TIME THEY CAN KILL US. SO LEAVE.

I DON'T WANT TO PUT YOU LOT IN DANGER. WATSON CAME IN FRONT. HE HELD HIS HAND AND SAID SOMETHING. I HAVE VERY BAD THINGS IN MY LIFE AND NOW I AM GETTING A GREAT OPPORTUNITY TO DO SO NICE WORK.

LIFE IS VERY SHORT. IT BEGINS WITH CRYING AND ENDS WITH CRYING. THIS

WORLD IS NOT OUR REAL HOME. WE DON'T KNOW WHO IS GOD. HE IS EVEN THERE OR NOT.

BUT WE WORSHIP HIM IN DIFFERENT NAMES. WE HAVE FAITH IN HIM. WE BELIEVE IN HIM. BECAUSE SOMEWHERE IN OUR BODY UNKNOWN THAT PART KNOWS THAT GOD IS THERE.

THESE ARE DARK TIMES. HE IS BACK. WE CAN GO INSIDE THAT DARK BUT WE SHOULD INSTEAD LIGHT A LAMP. WE NEVER DIE. THE PEOPLE LIKE OUR BEST FRIEND FRED WAS DEAD. BUT HE IS NOT DEAD.

HE HAS GONE TO HIS REAL HOME. I BELIEVE HE HAS GONE VERY FAR BUT HE IS STILL ALIVE FOR US BECAUSE HE IS IN OUR HEART.

BUT SATEN WILL DIE BECAUSE HE IS BAD AND HE HAS NO FRIENDS AND LOVE OF HIS FAMILY AND PEOPLE.

JAMES I AM READY TO DIE. IF YOU WILL SAY I'LL DIE JUST NOW I WILL DIE BECAUSE I WANT SUN TO KILL NIGHT. MOON ALWAYS GOES BUT THE SUN STAYS HERE.

THE WATER OF SEA IS SOUR BECAUSE IT TAKES AND IT IS STILL BUT THE WATER OF RIVER IS SWEET BECAUSE IT ALWAYS GIVE TO SEA AND KEEPS ON MOVING........... FIGHTING WITH DIFFICULTIES IN ITS WAY.

EVERY ONE CAME AND THEY HELD HIS HAND. WE ALL ARE WITH YOU.

OK, I FELT NICE TO HEAR THIS. AFTER AN HOUR, WE WILL LEAVE. WATSON AND CHRIS, GO AND START PACKING THE GUNS.

RONALD YOU STAY HERE..

THEY LEFT. IT WAS A JOURNEY FOR 1 HOUR. WHEN THEY WERE OUTSIDE THE PRISON, JAMES MADE EVERYONE INVISIBLE.

HE SAID STRAYED POINTING TOWARDS HIS AMOURS. THEY OPENED THE DOOR AND THEY SAW THAT ALL THE DEATHLY SPIRITS WERE SLEEPING.

HENRY'S ALL THE GUNS AND BOW AND ARROWS WERE HAVING A STICKY THING SO THAT THEY CAN BE STUCK TO THE WALL.

THEY PUT ALL THE MACHINE GUNS, HAND GUNS AND BOW AND ARROW EVERYWHERE.

THEY MADE ALL THE MACHINE GUNS BEND DOWN TOWARDS THE SPIRITS. AND THEN THEY MADE THE ROPES COME DOWN.

HIS GUNS WERE HAVING A ROPE SO THAT AS WE WILL PULL IT ALL THE BULLETS WILL START SHOOTING. HIS MACHINE GUNS AND HAND GUNS WERE HAVING 1000 BULLETS.

THE BOW AND ARROW HAD A SYSTEM THAT AS A ARROW WILL BE SHOOTED THEN A NEW ARROW WILL COME ON ITS OWN. THEY ALSO HAD ROPES.

ONE ROPE WILL ON 20 GUNS AND ARROWS. THE WORK WAS DONE. AND THEY WERE NOW VISIBLE. WATSON WAS STANDING NEAR A LADDER.

IN SHOCK THAT THEY HAD BEEN VISIBLE, WATSON BANGED WITH THE LADDER AND THE SOUND MADE THE SPIRITS WOKE UP.

ALL THE SHREWISH SPIRITS WOKE UP. GO RUN IN YOUR POCKET THERE WOULD BE A AMOUR WEAR IT FAST AND START PULLING THE ROPES.

DON'T CARE ABOUT ANYONE AND THE PERSON WHO IS INJURED. I AM

HERE FOR HIM. YOU HAVE TO FOLLOW MY INSTRUCTION.

JAMES WENT AT THE MOST BACK AND STARTED PULLING THE ROPE AND SOON IT LOOKED LIKE A PLACE OF WAR. BUT THEY WERE NOT INJURED BECAUSE JAMES KNEW THAT SOMETHING CAN HAPPEN LIKE THIS SO HE KEPT A PRECAUTION.

HE WAS RUNNING AND RUNNING. THE PRISON WAS BIGGER THAN A PROPER FOOTBALL FIELD. THE SPIRITS WERE COMING TOWARDS THEM. MOSTLY EVERYONE WAS DEAD BUT SOME WERE LEFT.

JAMES WAS SAVED MANY TIMES BY DOING A BROKEL. WATSON AND JOHN CAME OUT OF THE CAGE. THEN HE ALSO CAME. SO LETS MOVE ON. WAIT FOR A MINUTE WE JUST HAVE 3 PEOPLE WHERE IS CHRIS THEN HE QUICKLY RAN AND STOPPED WITH A JERK. OPEN THE GATE AS FAST AS YOU CAN! THEN HE SAW THAT 4 SPIRITS WERE AROUND CHRIS AND MOSTLY WERE DEAD. STRAYED, RIO TRISM HURRICUN, FRIOTRISM, STRAYED AND THEN EVERYONE WAS DEAD. BUT HE

DID LITTLE LATE, CHRIS WAS INJURED.
THEN HE PICKED HIM UP AND HE TOLD
THEM TO OPEN THE GATE AND THEN HE
THREW CHRIS OUT OF THE PRISON AND
THEN HE TOOK OUT A FIRST AID AND THAT
ALSO JAMES THREW. THE GATE WAS
OPENED AND THEN THE 3 SPRITS WHICH
WERE LEFT BECAUSE ALL THE ARMORS
WERE OVER, JUMPED ON HIM AND THEN
THEY RAN TO KILL HIM. ONE SPIRIT MADE
HIS HAND CURL AND A DANGEROUS LINE
CAM WITH A GREAT SPEED AND THEN
JAMES TRIED TO ESCAPE BUT THAT
LINE BANGED A LITTLE WITH HIS CORD
AND IT FELL ON THE FLOOR. HE TOLD
THEM TO SHUT THE DOOR. NO WE CAN'T
DO THIS. WHAT I AM SAYING THAT YOU
DO. THEN THEY STARTED SHUTTING IT.
HE QUICKLY PICKED UP HIS CORD AND
THEN JAMES LOOKED BACK AND HE SAW
THAT THE GATE WAS GOING TO CLOSE
THEN HE DODGED AND HE CAME OUT OF
THE PRISON. AS HE CAME THE 3 SPIRITS
BANGED AND THEN HE THOUGHT THAT
IF I WOULD HAVE DONE A SECOND ALSO
LATE THEN I WOULD HAVE BEEN DEAD.

THEY WERE BANGING SO MUCH THAT THE DOOR BROKE. THEN THEY RAN TO RESCUE THEMSELVES BUT WHEN THEY LOOKED BACK A WOHIMN WAS STANDING AND THE DOORS WERE CLOSED. AND THEN THEY LOOKED BACK AND OVER THERE ALSO A MAN WAS STANDING AND THEN THEY LOOKED RIGHT AND LEFT AND OVER THERE ALSO TWO HIMN WERE STANDING. THEN THEY TOOK OUT THEIR CORD AND CHRIS, JOHN AND WILLIAM WERE STANDING WITH THE THREE HIMN. THE THREE HIMN WERE HOLDING THEIR NECK. YOU LEAVE THEM OR I WILL KILL YOU. FOR THAT YOU HAVE TO FIGHT WITH HIM. THEN WE TOOK OUT OUR CORD. HE SAID 'RIOTRISM.' THAT WOMAN SAID 'GIORDRISK.' AND THEN I LOOSED. THEN THAT MAN COME AND THEN HE TOOK OUT HIS KNIFE AND AS HE WAS GOING TO STABLE IT A MAN COME FROM THE GROUND. HE HELD HIS HAND. STAY AWAY FROM HIS CHILD. THEN IN HIS MIND A WORD CLICKED 'FATHER.' DAD HOW ARE YOU HERE! JUST FOR YOUR PROTECTION HIS SON. DRIOFRIST AND THEN M ALL THE

FRIENDS WERE SAVED AND ALL THE 3
HIMN AND 1 WOHIMN WERE DEAD. THEN
I HUGGED HIS FATHER. CHILD I AM VERY
PROUD OF YOU. YOU STAY HERE AND WHEN
YOUR WHOLE WORK IS DONE YOU PROMISE
HIM THAT YOU WILL COME IN REDSCOUT.
EVERYONE IS WAITING FOR YOU. FATHER
I PROMISE YOU I WILL COME AN FATHER
DON'T TELL ANYONE WHERE I AM BECAUSE
I WANT TO GIVE THEM A SURPRISE.
OK JAMES NOW I AM GOING. BY. IF IN A
DANGER YOU TAKE THIS PHOTO. TAKE IT
AND JUST THINK ABOUT JESUS AND USE
THE BROKEL LIKE GIORDRISK. STRAYED,
CIUTRYUINDERESTED AND WHEN YOU
WANT TO KILL MANY OF THEM THEN USE
DRIOFRIST. THEN WE ALL COME BACK TO
OUR LAB. WE DID THE TREATHIMNT FOR
CHRIS AND THEN WE WENT FURTHER.

THIS IS THE MOST DEADLY AND FINAL
PLAN. THE PLAN IS VERY DANGEROUS.
AGAIN I AM SAYING LEAVE. BUT NONE DID
THIS. SEE FIRST I WILL GO. I WILL TAKE
THE GOLDEN BALL AND THEN AS HE WILL
BE GOING TO DO BROKEL I WILL MAKE
HIS BROKEL COME CONTACT WITH THE
GOLDEN BALL. AND I KNOW HE WILL NOT
LET THE BROKEL COME WITH THE GOLDEN
BALL. WE HAVE TO JUST NOW THINK THIS
ONLY THAT HE WILL NOT DO ANY TYPE
OF BROKEL. SO I WILL SAY HIM TO PUT
HIS CORD DOWN AND THEN RON YOU WILL
COME AND TAKE HIS CORD. AND I KNOW

THAT HE WILL FIGHT. I AM PRETTY GOOD IN FIGHTING SO NO PROBLEM. THEN I WILL CURISIFIE HIM AND THEN WE WILL TAKE ALL THE REVENGE. I WILL FORCE HIM TO SAY A BROKEL AND TAKE HIS CORD BACK. AS HE WILL SAY THIS WE WILL PUT THE GOLDEN BALL IN THE DIRECTION WHERE THE BROKEL IS COMING AND THEN SATEN IS DEAD. WE WILL ASK HIM THIS ALSO THAT WHERE IS CITRUS STONE. THEN WE WILL GO BACK IN TIME. BUT THE PROBLEM COMES IN THIS PLAN IS THAT THE GOLDEN BALL'S 7 PEOPLE WILL NOT KILL US. THEN THEY ALL SAT DOWN AND STARTED THINKING. THEN RON GOT AN IDEA. YES HE HAD AN IDEA. JAMES YOU WILL TELL SATEN THAT YOU ARE AFRAID SO THAT THE 7 PEOPLE CAN KILL YOU. THEN SATEN WILL ORDER THE BALL NOT TO COME OUT TILL THE TIME IT IS WITH HIM JAMES. YOU HAVE TO NOT GIVE IT TO ANY ONE. THAT'S BRILLIANT PLAN, RON. OK TOMORROW WILL BE THE FINAL DAY FOR OUR MISSION. EVERY ONE GETUP AT 8 AND WE WILL START IT. THEN THEY ALL WOKE UP. THIS IS THE WATCH THROUGH

WHICH YOU CAN TALK. HE TOOK HIS CORD AND THE SOME ARMORS AND JESUS'S PHOTO. THEN JAMES WENT ON WITHOUT TAKING ANY ONE. THEN HE REACHED FRIO'S OFFICE. SIR I AM HERE. TAKE THIS GOLDEN BALL. SIR I THINK THE 6 PEOPLE WILL KILL HIM. YOU HAVEN'T COME TO KILL HIM AND NONE WILL KILL YOU. SIR JUST FOR HIS SAFETY YOU CAN SAY TO THE GOLDEN BALL THAT TILL THE TIME IT IS IN HIS HAND THEN THE 7 PEOPLE SHOULD NOT COME OUT ALSO FROM THE BALL. OK, OK, OK. THEN HE SAID IT. THEN HE THREW TOWARDS HIM. HE JUMPED A LITTLE AND HE CATCHED IT. YOU WERE SAYING THAT I AM A FOOL BUT YOU ARE! WHAT DO YOU HIMAN? I HIMAN THIS. THEN HE TOOK OUT ALL HIS MAKEUP AND HIS CLOTHES AND A MASK. YOU BLOODY CHEATER. THEN HE TOOK OUT HIS CORD. DEGRST VIOREST GENED AND THEN ALL THE BOOKS ON THE SHELF STARTED FALLING ON HIM. FRICOUTRYIFRUST AND THEN A BROKEL COME TOWARDS HIM. HE SPRINTED SO HE WAS SAVED. THEN HE SAID GERDFRIST AND THEN

AGAIN A BROKEL COME TOWARDS HIM.
HE DODGED SO HE WAS SAVED. HE SAID
'LIOTWQXSZBV.' HE TOOK A CHAIR WHICH
HE GOT AND HE DID IT IN FRONT OF HIM.
BUT THE CHAIR BROKE AND THE BROKEL
HIT HIM SO BADLY THAT HE WENT FLYING
AND BANGED WITH A WALL. THEN HE
CAME TOWARDS HIM. THIS WILL BE YOUR
LAST BREATH AND THEN HE TOOK OUT
HIS CORD. NO YOU CAN'T SHOOT HIM. HE
DID THE GOLDEN BALL IN THE FRONT AND
THEN HE DID HIS CORD ASIDE. KEEP YOUR
CORD ON THE FLOOR. AND THEN HE TOOK
HIS CORD AND JAMES BROKE IT. THEN HE
BECAME SO MUCH ANGRY THAT HE TOOK
HIS CORD AND HE THREW IT VERY FAR.
THEN JAMES HELD HIS NECK AND HE
STARTED PUSHING HIM. THEN FROM HIS
RIGHT HAND HE BEAT HIM ON HIS HAND
AND HE MADE HIMSELF FREE. THEN HE
JUMPED VERY HIGH IN THE AIR AND THEN
HE BEAT HIM ON HIS FACE. HE HELD HIS
NECK AND THEN HE FELL ON THE FLOOR
WITH SATEN DOWN ABOVE HIM. THEN HE
DID A SNIPPING KICK AND HE FELL ON LAND.
THEN JAMES SAT ON HIM AND STARTED

PUNCHING HIM ON HIS FACE. THEN JAMES PICKED HIM UP WITH HIS COLLER AND STARTED ACTING LIKE A PROFESSIONAL BOXER. THEN HE GAVE HIM ON PUNCH AND THE OTHER AND HE BEAT HIM ON HIS FACE. HE THEN STOOD ON HIS BOTH THE HANDS AND THEN OVERLAPPED HIS NECK WITH HIS LEG AND THEN WITH HIS ALL POWER HE THREW HIM ON THE LAND. THEN HE RAN TOWARDS HIS CORD AND PICKED IT UP. AS HE PICKED IT UP SATEN CAME AND THEN HE PUSHED HIM AND THE CORD FELL. LETS END IT IN THAT WAY ONLY HOW WE STARTED. THEN HE HELD HIS NECK AND THEY FELL FROM THE HILL AS THEY WERE ON THE HILL. THEN THEY FELL ON THE GROUND THEY WERE BADLY INJURED. BUT THEY WERE NO DEAD BECAUSE THE PALACE WAS NOT ON THE TOP BUT IT WAS TOWARDS THE END AND THEY FELL ON SOMETHING THAT WAS FLUFFY. THEN THEY CRAWLED ON THE FLOOR TO REACH HIS CORD BUT HE TOOK IT FIRST. GIORDRISK AND THEN SATEN WAS ATTACHED WITH A TREE. THEN HE CALLED HIS ALL THE FRIENDS AND THEN

THEY STARTED BEATING SATEN. THEY
WERE SHOOTING HIM WITH THEIR BULLETS
AND IT WAS HARMING VERY MUCH SATEN
BECAUSE THE GOLDEN BALL WAS WITH
HIM AND HE HAD PUT BROKELEL POWER
IN IT. THEN HE GAVE HIM HIS CORD AND
HE HELD IT AND THEN THEY FORCED HIM
O SAY A BROKEL AND THEN HE SAID AND
THEN IT BANGED WITH THE BALL. BUT
NOTHING HAPPENED. YOU TELL US THE
REAL WAY TO DESTROY THE GOLDEN
BALL BUT HE JUST LAUGHED. THEN HE
TOOK A GUN AND HE SAID THAT I WILL
KILL HIM. AND THEN AS HE WAS GOING
TO SHOOT HIM SOMETHING HAPPENED. A
BULLET CAME AND IT MADE SATEN FREE
AND THEY LOOKED BACK AND SAW THAT
MAN WAS A WORKER OF SATEN AND
THEN JAMES SHOT HIM WITH HIS SHOTGUN
AT THAT MOHIMNT. THEN THEY LOOKED
IN THE FRONT AND JAMES SAW THAT
SATEN WAS STANDING ANGRILY AND HE
HAD A CORD WITH HIM. DFROHGYT AND
THEN HE IT BANGED WITH HIM AND HE
WAS DEAD. HE WAS NOT DEAD BUT HE
WAS JUST ACTING AND HE WAS SAVED

BECAUSE HE WAS HAVING VERY STRONG SHIELD. YOU CAN USE THE SHIELD WHICH THE PEOPLE OF THE PALACE WERE USING TO DEFEAT SATEN. SO HE WAS NOT DEAD. JAMES SPOKE A LITTLE IN A WAY THAT HE WAS DEAD. YOU LEAVE HIM TAKE THIS GOLDEN BALL RON AND LOOK AFTER ITS SAFETY. HE GAVE HIM IT IN A SMALL BAG MADE UP OF PURE COTTON. THIS IDEA HE APPLIED BECAUSE THAT TIME THE GOLDEN BALL WAS IN DANGER AND NO ONE WAS THERE TO SAVE IT. THEN RON TOOK IT AND THEY ALL RAN AND RAN IN THE FOREST. BY JAMES I WILL HIMET YOU IN REDSCOUT. HE KNEW THAT ALL OF THEM WILL DIE BUT HE WAS NOT DOING ANYTHING BECAUSE WITH THE HELP OF CITRUS STONE EVERYTHING WILL COME RIGHT AND IF I GO TO SAVE THEM THEN NOR I WILL ABLE TO FIND CITRUS STONE. SATEN WAS RUNNING AND THEN HE FOUND JOHN AND THEN HE STARTED ATTACKING HIM BUT HE WAS SAVED AND HE USE TO ALSO SHOOT HIM WITH THE GUN AND AT LAST HE WAS DEAD. HE WAS SEEING THIS ALL BECAUSE HE HAD PUT A COMERA IN

THEM. HE WAS FIRST ONLY KNEW THAT
EVERYONE WILL DIE AND SATEN WILL GET
THE GOLDEN BALL BUT HE WAS 50% SURE
THAT THE GOLDEN BALL WILL FINISH
AND HE WILL DIE. BUT WHEN THAT NEWS
TURNED INTO FAKE NEWS THEN I GOT TO
KNOW 100% THAT SATEN WILL GET THE
GOLDEN BALL.

HE HAS PRECAUTION AND THAT WAS
TO GO ON MARS. AFTER PLANTING THE
BOMB. AND HIS PLAN IS WHOLE DONE
ONLY. THEN I SAW THAT SATEN WAS
BACK OF CHRIS. SATEN WAS HAVING A
GUN WITH HIM WHICH WAS OF JOHN. CHRIS
WAS A LITTLE BOLD. HE HID SOMEWHERE
AND STARTED SHOOTING SATEN. BUT AT
LAST SATEN GOT TO KNOW WHERE HE
IS AND HE JUMPED OVER THERE AND HE
BIT CHRIS'S NECK AND THEN HE SHOT
HIM WITH THE GUN. THIS IS A NICE GUN,
I WILL HAVE IT FOR HIM. THEN HE RAN
BACK OF WATSON. WATSON WAS EASILY
KILLED BY ONE TIME'S ONLY TRY. THEN
HE AT LAST WENT FOR RON. BUT RON
WAS RUNNING VERY FAST AND HE WAS
NOT ABLE TO SEE HIM. THEN HE WENT

INSIDE. THEN MORE AND MORE AND MORE AND AT LAST IN THE MIDDLE. THEN HE SAW RON. HE WAS SITTING. AS HE SAW SATEN HE STARTED RUNNING AND THEN RAN MORE INSIDE. ANY ANIMALS THEY WOULD SEE THEY WOULD KILL IT AT THAT TIME ONLY. THEN THEY RAN MORE INSIDE AND THEN AT LAST IN THE END. OVER THERE RON FOUND A HOUSE. HE WENT IN IT AND THEN HE FOUND THAT NO ONE WAS THERE. BUT AFTER SOMETIME SATEN ALSO COME INSIDE IT. THEN THEY STARTED SHOOTING AS HIS CORD WAS BROKEN. THEY TOOK SOMETHING SAFETY AND STARTED SHOOTING. THEN AT LAST HE WAS ALSO KILLED. THEN HE COME OUT WITH A ASK AND HE MADE A CORD FROM THE TREE. THEN IT WAS WORKING ALSO. THEN HE COME BACK AFTER 5 TO 6 HOUR AND AS HE COME HE ROSE HIGH AND HE FELL ON THE GROUND AND AS HE FELL A BIG GATE OPENED AND HE WENT INSIDE IT. AS THE GATE WAS GOING TO CLOSE HE ALSO WENT INSIDE IT. AS I COME I SAW A VERY BIG BOOK AND A VEY BOOK WAS TOP ON IT AND THE ONE WAS SIDE

AND ONE WAS RIGHT. AND SIDE BY SIDE A VERY BIG STATUE OF A CREATURE WAS CREATED. AND I SAW THAT SATEN WENT AND A GADGET WAS THERE. IT WAS A GADGET THROUGH WHICH THE PARENTS CAN GET TO KNOW THAT THERE CHILD IS IN REDSCOUT OR NOT. YOU HAVE TO JUST TYPE HIS NAME. SATEN TYPED HIS NAME AND IT COME THAT MISSING FROM 1 MONTH. THEN SATEN WITH ANGER BROKE IT AND HE AGAIN WENT OUT AND HE ALSO. THEN HE SAW HIS ARMOR AND HE UNDERSTOOD EVERYTHING. HE BEAT WITH HIS LEG ON HIS ARMOR AND HE WENT. I WENT TOWARDS HIS LAB.

I COME IN HIS LAB. I WENT STRAIGHT TO HIS SECRET ROOM. IT WAS VERY DARK. I SWITCHED ON THE LIGHTS AND FRONT OF HIM WAS A BIG BLACK COLOR BAG. I OPENED IT AND HE TOOK OUT HIS GUN. IT WAS NOT A GUN BUT BOMB LAUNCHER. TEN BOMB OF THAT GUN CAN DESTROY!1/4 OF THE EARTH! HE WAS HAVING 41 BOMBS IN IT. ON THE OTHER SIDE SATEN WAS VERY ANGRY. HOW IT CAN BE. SO BIG MISTAKE HE DID. THEN HE TOOK A KNIFE AND HE KILLED 2 PEOPLE STANDING OVER THERE. CALL MAX AND THE OTHER 4 PEOPLE. THEN THEY ALL

COME. JUST BECAUSE OF YOU ALL IT HAS HAPPENED. HE HELD MAX' NECK. YOU WILL BE THE FIRST ONE TO DIE. TEN HE THREW HIM OUT OF THE PALACE FROM THE WINDOW. THEN HE TOOK A GUN AND SHOT THEM. TAKE THIS DEAD BODY AND GIVE IT TO BIRDS AND ANIMALS. CALL THE SECURITY GUARDS OF THE ENTRANCE. THEN THEY BOTH COME. I THINK YOU ARE KEEPING THE SECURITY RIGHT. IF YOU ARE KEEPING THE SECURITY NICE SO HOW JAMES AND HIS FRIENDS HAVE ENTERED THE PALACE? SIRR..R RR I DON'T KNOW HOW THEY ENTERED. THEN HE SLAPPED HIM TOW TIMES. SORRY SIR AGAIN THIS MISTAKE WILL NOT HAPPEN. SIR YOU HAVE CALLED HIM FOR SOME WORK, WHAT IS THE WORK? HE DID N'T HAD ANY WORK BUT GOD HAD SO I AM SENDING YOU BOTH WITH HIM. THEN HE SHOT THEM. THEN HE CALLED THE HEAD OF THE ARHIS. PREPARE FOR THE WAR AND TAKE BEST 1000 PEOPLE OUT FROM THAT ARHIS AND SEND TO HIM. ON THE OTHER SIDE HE TOOK HIS GUN AND I MADE HISSELF INVISIBLE AND THEN I COME NEAR THE

LAB. I STARTED PUTTING BOMBS AROUND. I PUT 4 BOMBS AROUND IT AND ONE BOMB IT THE PALACE. THAT BOMB CANNOT BE SEE BECAUSE IT IS VERY SMALL. THEN HE TOOK A AIRPLANE AND I WENT IN MANY COUNTRIES AND I FELLED A BOMB IN IT. AND THEN I WENT TO A PLACE WHERE I CAN GET A ROCKET. HE WAS KNOWING HOW TO DRIVE A ROCKET BECAUSE VERY FIRST HE WAS BORN ON EARTH AND AT THE OF 22 I STARTED LEARNING HOW TO GO IN SPACE BUT UNFORTUNATELY HE HAD TO GO IN REDSCOUT. HE WAS ON EARTH FOR 22 YEARS BUT HE WAS OF LESS YEAR ACCORDING TO REDSCOUT BECAUSE 1 MONTH OF REDSCOUT IS1 YEAR OF EARTH. NOW DON'T PUT VERY MUCH BRAIN. I MADE HIS LAB NEAR THE ROCKET AND THEN I HID IT WITH HIS BROKEL. AND I GOT A NEW CORD AS I MADE IT ON HIS OWN. I WORKED FLUENTLY. THEN I WENT TO SLEEP. ON THE OTHER SIDE SATEN MADE THOSE 1000 PEOPLE GO IN EVERY COUNTRY AND KILL THE PEOPLE. THEY WERE EXTREMELY FAST BECAUSE THEY HAD JET ENGINES. HIS

BOMB S WOULD BLAST AFTER 1 MONTH. THEN THE 1000 PEOPLE CAME AFTER 1 WEEK. BUT THEY HAD NOT KILLED 1000 PEOPLE. THEN SATEN SEND THEM AGAIN. AND AGAIN THEY CAME AFTER 1 WEEK AND BUT THEY HAD NOT KILLED 10 PEOPLE. SATEN BECAME VERY ANGRY BUT HE SEND THEM TO THE ARHIS. I WANT SOMEHOW THAT JAMES. TOMORROW I WILL SEND A PERSON TO FIND JAMES.

HE WAS TAKING A NICE SLEEP BUT HIS WONDERFUL SLEEP WAS BROKEN BY THE SOUND OF 10 PEOPLE. OUR LIFE IS IN VERY BIG DANGER. WE ARE GOING TO DIE. WE HAVE TO HIDE SOMEWHERE. WHO ARE YOU ALL? SEE, WE ARE THE LEFT SURVIVOR ON EARTH WHO ARE FIGHTING AGAINST EVIL. WHAT ARE YOU SAYING? SATEN SEND SOME PEOPLE AND THOSE PEOPLE KILLED EVERY ONE AND NOW JUST WE ARE LEFT AND TOMORROW THEY ARE AGAIN COMING AND THEY HAVE GOT THE NEWS THAT WHERE WE ARE. WE SHOULD HIDE. WAIT LET HIM THINK. AT THAT TIME ONLY ONE IDEA COME IN HIS MIND AND THAT WAS TO GO ON MARS. WE

WILL GO ON MARS. THIS IS NOT THE TIME FOR KIDDING. I AM NOT KIDDING! HE HAD A ROCKET WITH HIM AND I KNOW HOW TO FLY A ROCKET. THEN HE MADE HIS LAB A COMPRESSOR AND KEPT IT IN HIS POCKET AND THEY SAT IN THEIR ROCKET. ON THE OTHER SIDE SATEN SEND HIS ALL THE HIMMBER TO FIND THEM BUT THEY FAILED. THEN HE SEND SOME PEOPLE TO THE LOCATION WHERE HE LIVED FIRST. THEY FOUND THAT THERE WAS ROCKET AND SOMEONE HAS WENT OUT OF THE EARTH. THEN HE WENT RUNNING AND RUNNING TO SATEN. JUST 2 DAYS WERE LEFT TO BLAST. SIR THEY ARE NOT ON EARTH THEY HAVE WENT OUT. THEN ANOTHER PERSON COME. SIR HE HAVE PLANT BOMBS ON EARTH AND THEY WILL BLAST DAY AFTER TOMORROW. WHERE THEY WOULD HAVE WENT. I THINK ON MARS. YES WE WILL GO ON MARS. BUT HOW. FROM BROKEL. SAY EVERYONE TO TAKE A AXE AND CUT A WOOD LIKE THIS AND SOON ALL CORD WERE CREATED AND 1 DAY WAS LEFT FOR BLAST. THEN HE GAVE EVERYONE CORD AND HE SAID

A BROKEL AND IT AFFECTED ALL THE CORD. THEN HE ORDERED THEN TO SAY HIOADERS. AS THEY SAID THEY FLEW IN THE AIR AND THEN SATEN TOO. SATEN HAS BROUGHT 1000 PEOPLE FROM REDSCOUT WHO NOW BROKEL. ON THE OTHER HAND WAS SITTING IN HIS LAB AND THEN HE SAW AN U.F.O COMING. ON MARS. HE MADE EVERY ONE WAKE AND HE TOLD THEM TO TAKE THEIR GUNS AND HE TOOK HIS CORD. AND THEN THEY CAME OUT. FROM THAT U.F.O AN ALIEN CAME OUT. HE GAVE HIM A GADGET AND HE PRESSED THE BUTTON. WHAT ARE YOU DOING HERE? IT'S OUR AREA. GET AWAY FROM HERE OR I WILL SHOOT YOU. WE NEED YOUR HELP.

WHICH TYPE OF HELP? THEN I STARTED TELLING HIM HIS STORY. I MADE AN ELIXIR AND THEN TO TEST IT I PUT IT IN THE MOUTH OF THE MUMHIS. BUT I FORGOT TO PUT WC POWDER AND THEN THE MUMHIS STARTED DESTRUCTING THE WORLD. HE WAS KNOWING A MAN AND HIS NAME WAS OCKWILL AND I WANTED A HELP FROM HIM. ONE DAY HE WAS GOING TO TAKE A

HELP FROM HIM AND THEN WHEN HE WAS
CYCLING I SAW THAT THE MUMMIES WERE
THERE. THEY BEAT HIM VERY MUCH AND
THEN I SAW THAT THE MUMMIES WERE
HOLDING THEIR HAND AND THEY SAID
SOMETHING AND A MAN COME FROM THE
SKY. HIS NAME WAS SATEN. THEN I TOLD
HIM EVERYTHING ABOUT REDSCOUT. THEN
ONCE I HIMT SATEN AND OVER THERE
HE STARTED ATTACKING HIM AND THEN
MR. OCKWILL COME TO HELP. THEN I SAW
THAT HE WAS IN PRISON AND SOMEHOW
I ESCAPED FROM THERE WITH THE HELP
OF MR. OCKWILL AND THEN HE WAS DEAD.
THEN HE THOUGHT TO DEFEAT SATEN.
SO HE TOOK A HELP OF HIS 4 FRIENDS.
THEN I TOLD HIM THE STORY HOW THEY
WERE DEAD AND HOW WE COME HERE? I
AM READY TO HELP YOU BUT YOU HAVE
TO FIGHT WITH HIM. OK. THEN I WENT
BACK AND HE ALSO. STRAYED AND THEN
HE ALSO DID SOMETHING BUT I LOOSED.
FRIOTRISM AND THE HE WENT IN THE AIR
AND HE FELL ON THE LAND. HE WENT
TOWARDS HIM AND THEN HE PICKED HIM
UP. HE STARTED SAYING SOMETHING BUT

BY HIS ALL THE POWERS HE WAS SAVED. THEN HE SAID A BROKEL AND HE BANGED WITH HIS U.F.O. HE WENT TOWARDS HIM. HE PICKED HIM UP AND HE SAID STRAYED POINTING THE CORD TOWARDS HIS HAND AND HIS HAND BECOME BLUE. AND THEN I BEAT HIM WITH HIS HAND. HE WENT FLYING AND HE FALLED. THEN HE WENT RUNNING AND RUNNING AND THEN DID A B IN THE BROKEL AND THEN HE CAME AND SAID GIORDRISK POINTING THE CORD TOWARDS HIS BODY AND THEN HE DID A SNIPPING KICK AND HE LAID EXHAUSTED ON MARS. THEN HE TOOK HIS CORD AND I POINTED IT TOWARDS HIM. YOU WON. YOU ARE POWERFUL. I AM READY TO HELP YOU. THEN I PICKED HIM UP AND WE WENT IN HIS U.F.O. HIS U.F.O WAS SO BIG THAT HIS LAB ALSO COME INSIDE IT.

On that day only he was sitting out and then he saw that many people were coming and they were coming on Mars but they were not coming near them and then he got to know that they were Saten's arhis. He went running in the U.F.O. They are coming. Who are coming. Saten. Ok make every one ready. James you stay here only. Take this device. If we lose you pres this button and very much aliens will come. And take this also. If you will press this button the died aliens's

POWER WILL COME IN IT AND THEN FROM HERE A BULLET WILL COME. YOU FIX IT IN A GUN AND THEN SHOOT SATEN. OK, BY. THEN WE SAW THAT SATEN AND HIS ARHIS WAS COMING AND HIS ARHIS WAS GOING. THEN THEY STOOD WITH 12 FEET SPACE. THEN THEY STARTED THE WAR. BLOOD FELL, DEATH WAS THERE, EVEN THE ALIENS FAILED, ONE MAN HERE WAS DEAD AND THE OTHER WAS THERE DEAD. HE KILLED HIM WITH HIS CORD AND THE OTHER KILLED HIM WITH THEIR GUNS. IT WAS A TIME OF SORROW. IT WAS THE TIME OF DEATH. IT WAS THE TIME OF EVILS. IT WAS WORST THAN A WORLD WAR. IT WAS EXTREMELY BAD. HERE BLOOD, THERE BLOOD, THERE A MAN KILLED AND THERE A MAN FIGHTING. THE SURFACE OF MARS WAS COVERED WITH BLOOD. EVERYWHERE BLOOD. EVERY WHERE A PERSON KILLED. THEN HE SAW THAT THEY WERE LOOSING. SO HE QUICKLY CAME OUT AND MADE THE U.F.O INVISIBLE. THEN HE TOOK A MACHINE GUN AND HE ALSO STARTED SHOOTING. THEN IT WAS EQUAL. HE CAME BACK IN THE U.F.O AND AFTER SOMETIME

WE LOST BECAUSE ARE KING WAS DEAD AND EVERYONE WAS LEFT. SATEN'S ARHIS WAS WHOLE FINISHED BUT SATEN WAS LEFT. THEN SATEN TRIED TO FIND HIS U.F.O. WHERE IT IS? I WILL FIND IT LATTER. THEN I COME OUT AND HE TOOK ALL THE POWER BUT HE DID N'T MADE THE BULLET BECAUSE HE HAD TO TAKE THE POWER OF ALIENS IN SECOND WAR ALSO. THEN I STARTED CALLING THE OTHER ALIENS, AND ATLAST THEY COME. WE HAVE TO DO A WAR. BE READY AND GO FOR THE WAR. I WILL STAY HERE. THEN THEY STARTED THE WAR. WE THOUGHT THAT ALL THE PEOPLE OF SATEN WERE DEAD BUT HE WAS HAVING 1000 PEOPLE WHO KNOW BROKEL. THIS WAR WAS MORE DEADLY. BUT ALAS WE LOST. THEN HE COME OUT AND HE TOOK THE POWER OF THE ALIENS AND HE MADE IT BULLET AND HE PUT IT IN A MISSILE LAUNCHER AND THEN HE CAME OUT. HE SAW THAT SATEN WAS COMING FRONT OF HIM. HE WAS COMING LIKE A KING. JAMES HI. HOW ARE YOU. WHERE IS THE CITRUS STONE?

OK I WILL TELL YOU BUT IT WILL BE OF NO USE BECAUSE I WILL KILL YOU JUST NOW. IN HIS PALACE HIS CABIN IN THAT A SHELF IS THERE AND IN IT A DOOR IS THERE. IF YOU OPEN IT YOU WILL GET THE CITRUS STONE. THEN HE STARTED DOING BROKELS. I DODGED AND THEN SPRINT AND THEN DID SOME OTHER ACTIONS. THEN SATEN STARTED RUNNING ROUND OF HIM. HE RAN SO FAST THAT WHAT TO SAY. THEN HE STOPPED. AS HE STOPPED I RELOADED HIS GUN TO KILL HIM BUT THEN HE WAS NOT THERE. HE WAS BEHIND HIM. AS HE LOOKED BACK HE WAS NOT THERE. THEN HE LOOKED RIGHT AND HE WAS LEFT. THIS HAPPENED FOR AN HOUR AND THEN HE STARTED RUNNING ROUND OF HIM AGAIN. THEN HE CLOSED HIS EYES AND HE FOCUSED ON THE VOICE OF THE FOOT STEP. THEN HE LOOKED BACK AND AS HE WAS GOING TO SHOOT SATEN BECAME 10 AND THEY WERE STANDING ROUND OF HIM. THEY WERE SHOUTING, 'I AM SATEN, I AM SATEN.' HE CLOSED HIS EYES AND HE REMEMBERED THAT LAST

HE HAD HEARD THE SOUND BACK OF HIM AND HE SHOT SATEN, WHO WAS BACK OF HIM. THEN ALL SATEN WENT AND I SAT IN THE U.F.O AND I COME ON EARTH. I WENT TO HIS PALACE.

HE WENT TO HIS LAB. HE OPENED THE DOOR BUT HE DIDN'T FIND ANY SHELF. THEN HE SAW THAT SOME TYPE OF PAPER WAS PUT ON THE WALL. HE REMOVED IT AND HE FOUND A BOARD WHICH READ THE FOLLOWING INSCRIPTIONS:

"SAY HIORED SCOURTVFG XXADVFFN VBVTGTE GTREDS WOOGTBC XWDGKLUR FBKI TRFGHK VFEHYRT GHDHJ'

THEN HE SAID THOSE WORDS. AND THEN SHELF COME OUT. THEN HE THOUGHT TO GO IN THE ROOM WHERE I OT THE DIAMOND AND THE GLOBE. I WENT THERE AND I SAW THAT THE DIAMOND WAS STRAIGHT.

THEN I PICKED IT UP. AS I PICKED IT A ROPE COME AND IT MADE HIM COME IN THE AIR AND THEN IT STARTED BANGING HIM WITH THE WALL. FIT THEY BANGED HIM RIGHT THEN LEFT.

Then front then back. When he was banging him to right he found an axe and picked it up. And then he cut the rope and kept the diamond in his pocket. He picked up the globe and found a himtal which was in key's shape. As he touched it a rope came and it picked him up and then the floor opened and over there was 1 crocodile. Then he got to know that just now he will die because the rope was going to break. He shook himself and went right. He saw a roped which was tied with the rope.

HE OPENED IT AND THE ROPE BROKE.
THEN FLOOR CLOSED. THEN HE STARTED
FINDING A THING FROM WHICH THEY BOTH
COULD STICK. AND THEN HE FOUND A ROCK
AND ON THAT IT WAS WRITTEN HEODRUST
AND THEN HE PUT HIS HAND ON IT AND
A ROOM CAME. HE WENT INSIDE IT. AS
HE WENT MANY PEOPLE CAME TO KILL
HIM. BUT HE KILLED THEM ALL. THEN
HE SAW THAT VERY FAR WAS A GLUE.
HE WENT RUNNING AND HE PICKED IT UP.
BUT AS HE PICKED IT UP, HE CAME IN AIR
AND HE SAW THAT BACK OF HIM WAS A
KNIFE AND HE WAS GOING TO BANG WITH
IT, SO HE WILL BE DEAD. HE KNEW THAT
SOMETHING WOULD HAPPEN LIKE THIS SO
HE WAS CARRYING A KNIFE WITH HIM.
HE CUT THE ROPE AND HE CAME DOWN
HE. PICKED IT UP AND THEN THE ROOM
STARTED BREAKING. HE RUSHED OUT
AND HE CAME IN SATEN'S ROOM. HE STUCK
THEM AND THEN HE OPENED THE SHELF.
OVER THERE HE FOUND A STONE WHICH
WAS A DIAMOND. THEN HE PICKED IT UP
AND THEN THE WHOLE PALACE STARTED
FALLING. I COME OUT AND HE THOUGHT

IN HIS MIND TO GO AT THAT TIME WHEN HE GOT AN IDEA TO MAKE AN ELIXIR. HE STARTED ROLLING. IT WAS VERY SCARY AND VERY PAINFUL. THEN HE CAME AT THAT TIME. HE SAW THAT HE WAS SITTING ON A COUCH. HE CAME INSIDE HIMSELF AND THEN HE WENT ON THE ROOFTOP WITH HIS CITRUS STONE. JAMES STOOD ON THE RAILING. HE SPREAD HIS HANDS AND JUMPED. THEN AFTER 1 HOUR HE SAW THAT HE WAS LYING ON THE FLOOR AND MOM AND DAD WERE IN FRONT OF HIM." DAD AND MOM" HE HUGGED THEM. DAD I KILLED SATEN AND WHERE IS THE CITRUS STONE? YOU HAVE NOT KILLED SATEN. HE WAS JUST ACTING. HE TOLD HIS GOLDEN BALL THAT DON'T COME IN THE MIDDLE SO YOU GOT THE CITRUS STONE. KILLING SATEN IS NOT EASY. BUT YOU HAVE BROUGHT THE CITRUS STONE AND THAT WAS A THING FROM WHICH YOU WILL BE PRAISED WHOLE YEAR. BY THE WAY IT IS ON ITS RIGHT PLACE. WE HAVE TO GO FROM HERE. BUT WHY? PARENTS ARE NOT ALLOWED HERE AND WHEN THE HOLIDAYS COME YOU WILL COME TO

OUR REAL HOUSE. WHERE IS ROELD AND HALEN. THEN HE POINTED TOWARDS THEM. ROELD AND HALEN. I HUGGED THEM. SO HOW WAS YOUR ADVENTURE. WE WERE VERY MUCH ALONE WITHOUT YOU. WE HAVE TO TALK A LOT AFTER THE FEAST. THEN WE GOT A FEAST AND I GOT HIS REAL CORD THAT DON'T BREAK. THEN HE WAS SHOWN HIS ROOM. WE ALL THREE FRIENDS TALKED A LOT. I TOLD THEM WHAT IS ON EARTH AND HIS ADVENTURE AND THEY TOLD HIM ABOUT REDSCOUT. FROM THAT I GOT A VERY BAD NEWS AND THAT WAS THAT CHRISTINO IS ALSO IN REDSCOUT. HE HAD COME YESTERDAY ONLY. HE WAS VERY INJURED WHEN HE COME AND THAT WAS BECAUSE ON HIS WAY HE SOMEHOW GOT A ACCIDENT AND JUST NOW HE IS IN HOSPITAL WHICH IS IN REDSCOUT. THEN WE ALL SLEPT.

Get up Henry. It is the class of Madam Jessica. If you are late, she will kill you. A boy with long nose, shining eyes, big black hair was banging a pillow on Henry's face. James just shook his hand and then he again slept. Let me sleep Roeld, I have not slept from a week.

'But it is the class your first class. I think Madam will come and make you wake up. Oh! Madam Jessica is not going to come here. I am not a celebrity. No! Not Madam, Halen. Just then a voice came from the

DOOR. WHAT YOU ALL ARE DOING. WEAR YOUR HOODS, WE HAVE TO GO.

AND JAMES YOU ARE SLEEPING, GET UP FAST. JAMES WOKE UP TIRELESSLY. HALEN WAS ALREADY READY WITH HER PING HOOD AND ROELD TOO. JAMES WORE HIS HOOD AND WENT TO TAKE HIS BOOKS. 'NO, YOU HAVE TO NOT TAKE YOUR BOOKS' SAID HALEN. YOU HAVE TO TAKE JUST YOUR CORD. BUT I DON'T KNOW ANY BROKELS. MADAM JESSICA WILL TELL YOU. JAMES TOOK HIS CORD AND WENT TO THE CLASS. THEY TALKED ALL THE WAY BUT THEN SOMEONE PUSHED THEM. HE WAS CHRISTINO.

SO HOW YOU ARE FEELING, ALBUS. GET AWAY. HALEN PUSHED HIM. JAMES WENT FROM THERE. CHRISTINO WAS LAUGHING. FINALLY THEY REACHED THE CLASS. IT WAS VERY BIG CLASS. THERE WERE ANIMALS IN GLASSES ALL AROUND.

THERE WAS A SOUND OF MURMURING. THEY TOOK THEIR SEATS AND FROM THE PASSAGEWAY, MADAM JESSICA CAME. SHE WAS AN OLD WOMAN WHO WAS WEARING SMALL GLASSES. SHE

WAS WEARING A GREEN GOWN. SILENCE, EVERYBODY KEEP QUIET.

TODAY WE ARE GOING TO LEARN NEW BROKELS. FIRST ONE IS MOCKMILLON. EVERYBODY REPEAT. EVERYBODY STARTED SAYING THE BROKEL. IT IS NOT MOCKMILLEN, IT IS MOCKMILLON.

SIR RETROT WILL TELL YOU ABOUT IT. FROM THIS BROKEL, YOU CAN RAISE A PERSON. SHE TOOK AN INSECT FROM A GLASS AND PLACED IT ON THE TABLE. LOOK TOWARDS ME.

SHE TOOK HER CORD AND POINTED IT TOWARDS THE INSECT. SHE SHOUTED 'MOCKMILLON.' BUT NOTHING HAPPENED. THEN SHE RAISED HER CORD, THE INSECT WAS ALSO FLYING. NOW WE WILL GO FOUR STEPS BACK AND AGAIN I WILL SAY MOCKMILLON.

SHE WENT FOUR STEPS BACK AND AGAIN SHE SHOUT MOCKMILLON. AS SHE SAID, THE INSECT WENT BACK IN GREAT SPEED AND BANGED WITH THE WALL.

NOW WE WILL GO TOWARDS HIM AND SAY REDCLIF. SHE WENT TOWARDS THE INSECT AND SAID REDCLIF BUT NOTHING

HAPPENED. NOTHING WILL HAPPEN TO HIM BECAUSE HE DOESN'T HAVE A CORD.

IF YOU SAY THIS BROKEL ONLY WITH THIS PROCESS, THE OPPONENT'S CORD POWER WILL BECOME JUST 5%.

IF SOMEONE IS ATTACKING YOU WITH THIS BROKEL SO YOU CAN USE A BROKEL NAMED QUICK FREE. I WILL MAKE YOU UNDERSTAND. SHE WENT ON THE BLACKBOARD AND DREW SOMETHING. IT WAS THE ENTIRE THING WHICH SHE HAS TAUGHT THEM JUST NOW. NOW YOU ALL HAVE TO PRACTICE. SHE POINTED HER CORD IN THE SKY AND SAID SOMETHING. SOON THE CLASS TURNED INTO A MAZE. A VOICE CAME FROM BACK. YOU HAVE YOUR OPPONENTS IN THE FRONT. WHO SO EVER WILL WIN, WOULD GET GIFT. GOOD LUCK!

JAMES LOOKED IN THE FRONT AND SAW THAT IT WAS CHRISTINO. AS JAMES WAS GOING TO SAY SOMETHING, CHRISTINO STARTED ATTACKING. HE HID BEHIND A WALL. CHRISTINO WAS LOOKING HERE AND THERE. WHEN CHRISTINO WAS LOOKING BACK, JAMES CAME OUT AND

SAID 'MOCKMILLON.' CHRISTINO RAISED INTO THE AIR. JAMES WENT BACK AND SHOUTED MOCKMILLON. CHRISTINO WENT BACK WITH A GREAT SPEED.

THE WALL CRACKED. AS JAMES WAS GOING TO SAY REDCLIF, CHRISTINO SAID A BROKEL. JAMES WENT FLYING AND BANGED WITH THE WALL. THEY BOTH HID SOMEWHERE AND EVERY SECOND THEY USE TO ATTACK. CHRISTINO SAID A BROKEL AND HENRY'S PROTECTION BROKE. JAMES WAS RUNNING TO SAVE HIS LIFE.

JAMES SAID 'GEODEST' AND EVERYTHING STARTED TURNING INTO ASHES. JAMES RAN TO SAVE HIS LIFE. IT STARTED RAINING. THUNDERS WERE FALLING. THEN ALL OF A SUDDEN, EVERYTHING STOPPED. THERE WAS A COLD WING AND SOMEONE HELD HENRY'S HAND. HE LOOKED BACK TO SEE, HE WAS SATEN...... WITHOUT SAYING ANYTHING, SATEN STARTED ATTACKING HENRY. HE MADE A BIG FIRE BALL AND THREW IT TOWARDS HENRY. JAMES WENT FLYING AND BANGED WITH THE WALL. JAMES GOT

UP AND SAID 'MOCKMILLON.' BUT NOTHING HAPPENED. IT IS A BABY BROKEL. HE DID HIS HAND FRONT AND A BLUE LINE CAME FROM IT. JAMES ROSE INTO THE AIR. HIS BODY WAS PAINING VERY BADLY. HE THREW JAMES ON THE FLOOR. THE LIGHT WAS STILL COMING FROM HIS HAND. HE POINTED HIS HAND TOWARDS THE SKY. AFTER SOMETIME HIS FINGERS TURNED BLUE. HE WENT TOWARDS HENRY. HE ATTACHED HIS FINGERS ON THE STOMACH OF HENRY.

THE LIGHT WAS ELECTRICITY AND THAT TOO OF 10000S VAULT. JAMES WAS DYING WITH PAIN. HE PUSHED SATEN AND RAN TO SAVE HIS LIFE. BUT WHEN JAMES HAS RUN A LITTLE BIT, HE BECAME STATUE.

HE WAS NOT ABLE TO MOVE A BIT.

SATEN SAID SOMETHING TO HENRY. WHATEVER IS HAPPENING, YOU ARE NOT GOING TO TELL ANYONE OR YOUR FAMILY WILL BE DEAD.

HE SAID A BROKEL AND A SCARLET RED THING CAME FROM HIS MIND AND ATTACHED WITH HENRY'S. FROM THIS

BROKEL ANYONE CAN TAKE ANYONE BRAIN.

JAMES PICKED UP A STONE AND THREW IT ON SATEN. THE BROKEL BROKE THE WALLS AND WENT SOMEWHERE ELSE. SATEN SAID A BROKEL FROM WHICH THE BROKEL IS NOT SEEN AND ALL THE DESTRUCTION BECOMES OK. AFTER A MINUTE THE BROKEL CAME BACK AND HIT HENRY. JAMES ROSE INTO THE AIR AND STARTED SHOUTING VERY BADLY. A YELLOW THING CAME FROM HIS BODY. IT WENT UP AND UP. BANG! JAMES FELT UNCONSCIOUS. JAMES WOKE UP. HE SAW JESUS CHRIST. HENRY, I AM JESUS CHRIST. I HAVE COME HERE TO TELL YOU THAT YOU HAVE GOT POWERS AND YOU HAVE TO USE IT WHEN IT IS NEEDED. YOU CAN'T USE YOUR POWER WHEN IT IS NOT NEEDED. HE GAVE HIM A WATCH. IF YOU TOUCH THIS WATCH, YOU WILL GET SOME SUITS WHICH WILL HELP YOU. YOU CAN'T TAKE YOUR WATCH OUT AFTER YOU HAVE WORN IT. YOU HAVE TO SAVE THE WORLD. YOU ARE NOW THE 1ST PERSON WHO CAN USE MARVELLE LOCKET. YOUR SUIT CAN

STOP THE DEVILS FOR A MINUTE BUT MARVELLE LOCKET CAN KILL THEM. AFTER SAYING THIS, HE DISAPPEARED. JAMES WENT MAD. HE WAS NOT ABLE TO BELIEVE TO ANYTHING.

FROM HIS WATCH A SOUND CAME. IT SAID THAT THE WORLD IS IN DANGER. JAMES PRESSED HIS WATCH AND A YELLOW LIGHT CAME OUT FROM IT. HE HANDS WAS COVERED WITH MANY GADGETS. HE WORE A HELMET. HIS KNEES WERE COVERED WITH A STEEL LOOKING PROTECTION. NOTHING ELSE WAS THERE AS PROTECTION.

JAMES LOOKED TOWARDS HIS SUIT AND HE PRESSED A BUTTON ON WHICH A ROCKET WAS MADE. HE DIDN'T FLY BUT HE TRANSPORTED. HE FELL ON THE LAND. IT WAS A PLACE WITH LOTS OF BUILDING. THE WEATHER WAS SUNNY. JAMES GOT UP. NO ONE WAS THERE. AS HE GOT UP, SOMEONE STARTED ATTACKING. A GREEN LINE CAME AND HIT HENRY. THIS HAPPENED FOR 5 TIMES. AFTER THAT JAMES STARTED USING HIS CORD. HE TOOK OUT A CORD FROM HIS POCKET

A MAN WITH PEAKY FACE, LONG NOSE, BRIGHT EYES, LONG HEIGHT AND LOOKING OLD WAS ATTACKING HENRY.

JAMES BEND HIS HEAD TO BE SAVE FROM BROKEL. HE TRIED IT FOR SOMETIME BUT THE BROKEL HIT HENRY.

JAMES WENT FLYING IN THE BUILDING. ONE MORE BROKEL HIT HIM, HE FELL FROM THE BUILDING, BUT HE WAS SAVING BECAUSE HE HAD USED HIS SUIT. A BROKEL AGAIN HIT HENRY. HE BROKE THE WALL OF THE HOUSES.

THAT MAN WAS CONTINUOUSLY DOING BROKEL. JAMES WENT FLYING IN A HOUSE. NO ONE WAS THERE. JAMES GOT UP. HE PRESSED A BUTTON IN HIS SUIT. FROM THAT A FAN CAME.

NOW WHENEVER HE USE TO DO A BROKEL, THAT FAN USE TO CUT IT. BUT UNFORTUNATELY HIS FAN BROKE. THAT MAN WORE A LOCKET. ON WHICH HIS NAME WAS WRITTEN. HIS NAME WAS DRAKE. DRAKE MADE A FIREBALL AND THREW AT HENRY. JAMES SAW A BUTTON LIKE THAT FIRE BALL ONLY. HE PRESSED IT. TWO HANDS CAME OUT AND HELD THE

BALL. IT WENT BACK INSIDE. THE BALL REFLECTED AND WENT BACK TO DRAKE.

THERE WAS ONE MORE BUTTON. ON THAT A HAND WAS MADE.

HE PRESSED IT. HIS HAND WENT RED. HE REMEMBERED THAT THIS THING WAS USED BY SATEN.

JAMES PUNCHED DRAKE. DRAKE WAS IN THE SKY. HIS LEG HAD ALSO TURNED BLUE. WHENEVER HE USED TO USE HIS LEGS OR HANDS, IT USE TO TURN RED OR BLUE.

JAMES HAS ATTACKED DRAKE FOR 5 TIMES. AFTER THAT HE MADE FIRE.

FIRE WAS COMING OUT FROM HIS HAND.

JAMES WAS JUMPING, BENDING. SPRINTING AND DOING OTHER ACTIVITIES TO SAVE HIS LIFE.

DRAKE SLAPPED HIM. JAMES WAS LYING ON THE GROUND.

HE MADE JAMES LEVITATE AND THREW HIM. JAMES BANGED WITH THE WALL. BLOOD WAS COMING FROM HIS HEAD. HIS FACE WAS COVERED WITH DUST. HIS CLOTHES HAD BECOME DIRTY.

NOW WHENEVER DRAKE USE TO SHAKE HIS HAND. JAMES USE TO GO IN THAT DIRECTION ONLY. JAMES ROLLED, JUMPED. WALKED, BANGED WITH THE WALL, BROKE 35 MIRRORS, MADE A BIG HOLE IN THE GROUND AND LAID ON THE GROUND. JAMES HAS DONE THIS ALL. HE WAS INJURED BADLY.

HE SAW A BLADE IN HIS HAND. IN WAS WRAPPED WITH SOME STRINGS ON HIS HAND. HE TOOK IT OUT. IT WAS VERY BIG.

THERE WERE FOUR BLADES, TWO IN EACH HAND. HE TOOK OUT TOW BLADES. HE RAN AS FAST AS HE COULD. DRAKE THREW AN ICE BALLS BUT JAMES WAS WENT AWAY FROM THE WAY. HE CLIMBED UP A LONG STOOL AND JUMPED. HE STUCK THE BLADE IN DRAKE'S NECK. HE STUCK ANOTHER ONE. BLOOD WAS COMING OUT FROM HIS NECK.

HE THREW HENRY. JAMES ROLLED IN THE SKY AND FELL ON THE LAND. THERE WAS A MANUAL SCRIPT. IT WAS WRITTEN HELP. JAMES PRESSED THE WIND BUTTON. THE DUST ON THE GROUND ROSE AND CREATED AN ATMOSPHERE.

JAMES WENT IN THE BUILDING. HE HID IN THE ROOM. HE OPENED THE SCRIPT. IT WAS WRITTEN THAT PUT 3 BLADES IN THE NECK OF DRAKE. HE WILL NOT DIE BUT HE WILL BE UNCONSCIOUS. IF HE PUT ONE BLADE IN YOUR NECK, YOU WILL BE UNCONSCIOUS.

SOMETHING ELSE WAS WRITTEN DOWN BUT HE COULD NOT READ IT BECAUSE DRAKE STARTED ATTACKING. JAMES GOT OUT FROM THE BUILDING. HE SAW THAT ONLY ONE BLADE WAS LEFT WITH HIM.

THE OTHER ONE WAS WITH DRAKE. HE WAS HOLDING THE BLADE IN HIS RIGHT HAND. JAMES RAN AND STUCK THE BLADE IN DRAKE'S NECK. BUT AT THAT TIME ONLY, DRAKE ALSO STUCK IT ON THE NECK OF HENRY. JAMES PUT HIS HAND ON HIS HEAD AND HE FELL ON THE LAND.

HE OPENED HIS EYES. BUT HE WAS NOT IN THAT PLACE. IT WAS A DARK ROOM WITH A LIGHT BULB WHICH GAVE LIGHT TO A VERY SMALL PORTION OF THE ROOM. A SCARLET GOLDEN POT WAS KEPT FRONT OF HENRY. THERE WERE TWO WINDOWS WITH A ROOM. IT WAS LOCKED.

JAMES WAS SITTING ON A WOODEN CHAIR. HIS HANDS WERE TIED WITH THE TWO ARMS OF THE CHAIR. JAMES STARTED SHAKING HIS HANDS. LEAVE ME.

WHO ARE YOU? AS HE SAID THIS, 10 CORD WERE PUT NEAR HIS HEAD. HE LOOKED AROUND AND FOUND 10 MEN WITH CORDS. JAMES WAS SPEECHLESS.

HE SAT LIKE A STATUE FOR A MINUTE. A MAN CAME FROM THE DOOR. HE WAS LOOKING VERY RICH. HE WAS WEARING A BLACK SUIT WITH BLACK POLISHED SHOES. HE HAD A FINE BLACK MOUSTACHE.

HE HAD BLACK EYES. HE LOOKED LIKE A GENTLEMAN. HIS HEIGHT WAS ALSO NICE.

JAMES COOK! HELLO! I AM FRIEK GREF. I AM ONE OF THE IMPORTANT MAN OF SATEN. YOU KNOW WHAT HAS HAPPENED? YOU EVEN DON'T KNOW WHAT IS GOING TO HAPPEN.

YOU KNOW WHAT MARVELLE LOCKET IS. OH! YOU WOULD NOT KNOW. FROM THAT LOCKET, ANYONE CAN BECOME VERY POWERFUL. IN THAT WORLD'S MOST

POWERFUL BROKEL ARE WRITTEN. BUT TWO PEOPLE ONLY CAN HAVE IT. ONE WAS SATEN.

THERE ARE 2 LOCKETS. ONE HAS 30% MOST POWERFUL BROKELS AND ONE HAVE 70%. 30% IS VERY MUCH BECAUSE THE BROKELS WHICH ARE MOST POWERFUL AND ARE NOT WRITTEN IN THAT LOCKET HAVE JUST 2% POWER. SATEN HAVE THE 70% ONE LOCKET.

HE WANTS THE SECOND ALSO. ANYONE CAN WEAR IT BUT JUST TWO PEOPLE CAN USE IT. A MAN WILL GET THE OTHER MAN'S LOCKET IN ONE CONDITION AND THAT IS, IF THAT MAN GIVE HIM.

THAT'S WHY TILL NOW THAT PERSON IS NOT DEAD. WE HAVE SEEN THE PERSON WHO HAS IT. THAT PERSON IS YOU. YOU ARE THE 2 MOST POWERFUL PEOPLE.

THAT POT YOU ARE SEEING. THAT, GOLDEN ONE.

WE CAN'T TAKE THE MARVELLE LOCKET FROM YOU. YOU KNOW WHAT THIS GOLDEN POT DOES? IF I WILL KILL YOU AND PUT YOU ON THE POT, YOUR SOUL

WILL GO INSIDE IT. AND WE WILL GET THE LOCKET. BUT ONE PROBLEM IS THERE.

YOU WANT TO SEE. HE WENT CLOSER TO THE POT. AS HE TOUCHED IT, IT VANISHED. I CAN'T TOUCH IT. JUST THE PEOPLE WHO HAVE TRANSPARENT HEART CAN TOUCH IT. THAT'S WHY WE ARE MAKING A FORMULA FROM WHICH WE CAN TOUCH IT.

TILL THE TIME WE DON'T GET IT, YOU WILL BE HERE. TOMORROW SATEN WILL COME AND HE WILL KILL YOU. AFTER SAYING THIS ALL HE WENT FROM THERE. AFTER TWO THREE MINUTE JAMES SLEPT.

9 HOURS HAVE PASSED AND IT WAS MIDNIGHT. JAMES WOKE UP. ALL THE 10 PEOPLE WERE ASLEEP. HE PRESSED HIS WATCH. THIS TIME HE GOT ANOTHER COSTUME. IT WAS OF BLACK COLOR. THERE WAS A MASK OF BLACK COLOR ON HENRY'S FACE. THE ODDEST THING WAS THAT HE HAS BECOME ADULT.

WHEN HE WAS FIGHTING DRAKE THEN ALSO HE WAS ADULT BUT HE DIDN'T NOTICE. HE GOT FREE FROM THE ROPES. AS HE STOOD, EVERYONE ASLEEP WOKE UP. JAMES RAN AND PICKED UP A ROD.

HE STARTED BEATING EVERYONE WITH IT. HE BEAT THE 1ST PERSON, 2ND PERSON AND THEN THE 3RD ONE. WHEN HE WAS BEATING A PERSON, SOMEONE HIT HIM ON HIS HEAD.

HE FELL ON THE GROUND. IN A SECOND EVERYONE HAD CIRCLED HIM. THEY WERE POINTING THEIR CORD TOWARDS HENRY.

THERE WAS A BUTTON ON HENRY'S SUIT. HE PRESSED IT. 10 ROPES CAME OUT WITH A SWORD ATTACHED TO IT IN THE END. IT WENT STRAIGHT AND HIT THE NECK OF EVERYONE. THEY FELL ON THE LAND.

THAT WAS A NICE MOVE. NOW HOW TO GO OUT. JAMES OPENED THE DOOR.

THERE WERE 3 PEOPLE. A PERSON TURNED TOWARDS HIM. AS HE TURNED, JAMES SHOUTED REDCLIF. THE PERSON ALSO TURNED. REPITCULOUS STRAYED. THEY WERE LYING ON THE FLOOR. IT WAS A ROOM WITH ONE DOOR.

JAMES OPENED THE DOOR. IT WAS A VERY SMALL ROOM WITH NO DOOR. WHAT TO DO NOW?

JAMES TOUCHED A WALL. AS HE TOUCHED IT, SOMETHING APPEARED. IT WAS SOMETHING ON WHICH WE HAVE TO PUT THE HAND.

ON HENRY'S SUIT A BOOK CAME. HE STARTED READING IT. IT SAID THAT THERE IS A BUTTON IN HIS SUIT WHICH IS OF COLOR. IF HE PRESSES IT THEN A BLUE LIGHT WILL COME AND WILL SCAN THE PLACE.

THERE WILL BE SOME MARKS OF THE HAND. HE HAS TO GO NEAR IT AND PUT THE PAPER WHICH IS IN HIS SUIT. WHEN HE WILL PUT IT, THE FINGERPRINTS WILL COME ON THE PAPER.

HE HAS TO THEN PUT THE PAPER ON THE THING ON WHICH A HAND IS MADE. JAMES DID EXACTLY LIKE THIS. A DOOR CAME. HE WENT INSIDE IT.

IT WAS THE TERIST. HE WENT CLOSE TO THE RAILING. HE PRESSED HIS FLYING BUTTON AND CAME IN REDSCOUT.

As he entered in his room, Halen came. Where were you? In the school only. Don't say lie. What do you think? From two days you were not there. Not attending your classes, from two days absent, where were you? I was here only. From two days, we come over here every hour and you are saying that you were here.

We even went to your house. Whole Redscout, we have searched for you.

From the door Roeld came. Yes, James where were you? I have to go.

WHERE? TO MY FATHER'S HOUSE. BUT IT
IS NIGHT. SO WHAT.

JAMES CAME OUT OF REDSCOUT AND
WENT TO HIS HOUSE.

JAMES KNOCKED ON THE DOOR. HENRY'S FATHER, THOMAS ALBUS CAME OUT. OH! JAMES WHERE WERE YOU? YOU FRIENDS CAME TO FIND YOU HERE.

WHERE IS MOM? SHE HAS GONE TO HER MOTHER'S HOUSE.

FATHER, I WANT TO ASK YOU SOMETHING? ASK MY DEAR. WHAT IS MARVELLE LOCKET? WHO TOLD YOU ABOUT IT? THEN JAMES TOLD HIM EVERYTHING WHAT HAS HAPPENED WITH HIM.

100 YEARS BACK. A CONSTITUTION WAS MADE. WHICH CONSTITUTION? THE

COMPANY BROUGHT THE MOST GENIUS PEOPLE WHO CAN MAKE BROKELS.

IT WAS A TEAM OF 1000 PEOPLE. THEY MADE THOSE BROKELS. THEY PUT THEM IN THE MARVELLE LOCKET.

BUT THEN A PROBLEM CAME. THEY TRIED TO DO THOSE BROKELS BUT THEY WERE NOT ABLE TO DO IT.

SCIENTIST FOUND OUT THE REASON. THEY SAID THAT, THAT PERSON ONLY CAN USE IT, WHO HAVE SO MUCH POWERS LIKE THE LOCKET.

THEY EVEN SAID THAT THE PERSON WHO IS BORN AFTER 64 YEARS ON 9 FEBRUARY AND 120' CLOCK CAN ONLY DO THESE BROKELS. THEY DIVIDED THE LOCKET IN TWO PARTS. ONE WHICH HAVE 30% OF POWER AND ONE WHICH HAVE 70% OF POWERS.

I AM NOT ABLE TO UNDERSTAND THIS % THING.

WHEN THEY COMPARED THE POWER OF THE LOCKET AND THE MOST POWERFUL BROKEL LEAVING THE BROKELS IN THE LOCKET, THEY SAW THAT THE MOST

POWERFUL BROKEL HAVE JUST 1% POWER COMPARING THE LOCKET.

YOU CAN IMAGINE, HOW MUCH POWERFUL THE LOCKET IS. SO ANYONE WAS NOT BORNE AFTER 64 YEARS.

YES! HE WAS BORN. WHO WAS HE?

YOU'RE GRANDFATHER. YES, YOU'RE GRANDFATHER.

JAMES GOT A BIG SHOCK AFTER THIS SENTENCE.

AND AFTER THAT SATEN WAS BORN.

SATEN GOT THE 70% ONE LOCKET. WHO WAS BORN AFTER SATEN? HENRY, YOU WERE BORN. ARE YOU NOT KIDDING? NO, YOU ARE THE PERSON WHO SHOULD GET THE LOCKET. SO WHO HAVE THE LOCKET?

YOUR GRANDFATHER GAVE ME THE LOCKET. AND NOW I AM GOING TO GIVE YOU.

HE TOOK OUT A GOLDEN LOCKET FROM HIS NECK. WEAR IT HENRY. JAMES WORE THE LOCKET.

USE IT WELL. FATHER ONE MORE QUESTION. WHY FROM SO MANY YEARS, ANY OTHER MARVELLE LOCKET WAS NOT MADE.

BECAUSE THE OWNER DID A BROKEL SO THAT ANYONE ELSE CAN'T MAKE IT.

WHY? SATEN IS CALLED 'DARK PRINCE'. BECAUSE THE CONSTITUTION SAID THAT THE PERSON WHO WILL BE HAVING THE LOCKET WILL BE CALLED THE PRINCE AND THE PERSON WHO WILL BE HAVING BOTH THE LOCKETS WILL BE CALLED THE KING. SATEN WAS CALLED DARK PRINCE BECAUSE HE WENT BAD.

FATHER I HAVE ONE MORE QUESTION. OK! BUT AFTER THIS NO MORE QUESTION. WHY THE GOLDEN POT WAS MADE? IT WAS MADE FOR SATEN. SO THAT THEY CAN TAKE THE MARVELLE LOCKET.

THANK YOU! FOR TELLING ME THE DETAILS.

BY! I HAVE TO GO NOW. EAT THE DINNER AT LEAST! THANKS, BUT I HAVE TO GO. JAMES FLEW INTO THE AIR AND WENT TO REDSCOUT.

HE WENT TO HIS ROOM AND SLEPT. THE NEXT MORNING HE WOKE UP. HE SAW THAT THERE WAS SNOWFALL. THE CLIMATE WAS DAME CHILL.

JAMES WENT TO THE WINDOW AND STARTED SEEING THE SNOWFALL. IT WAS NOT JUST A MINUTE WHEN HALEN CAME. JAMES I HAVE TO TELL YOU SOMETHING. WHAT? TOMORROW IS YOUR EXAMINATION. TODAY IS OUR HOLIDAY TO PREPARE.

'WHICH EXAMINATION' SAID JAMES IN A TONE OF HORROR? IT IS THE EXAMINATION OF BROKELS. YOU HAVE TO FIGHT WITH SOMEONE. YOU HAVE TO FIGHT WITH CHRISTINO. I AM NOT GOING TO FIGHT WITH CHRISTINO. YOU HAVE TO. BUT...I... HALEN WENT FROM THERE IGNORING HENRY. HALEN WENT FROM THE DOOR. BUT AFTER A SECOND SHE RETURNED BACK.

SHE PEEPED FROM THE DOOR. HEADMASTER IS CALLING YOU. OK! I AM GOING.

JAMES MADE HIS WAY TO THE OFFICE. AFTER A LONG SEARCH HE FOUND IT.

HE ENTERED IN IT.

HIS OFFICE WAS VERY BIG. IT WAS HAVING 7 TO 8 SHELVES WITH BOOKS. THERE WAS A PARROT IN A GOLDEN

CAGE. HIS ROOM WAS FILLED WITH LOTS OF ANTIQUE AND VINTAGE THINGS.

JAMES SHOUTED, SIR DAIFOI. IN A MINUTE, A MAN WITH LONG HEIGHT, A PALE FACE WITH A BEARD. HE WAS WEARING A VELVET RED GOWN. HE WORE A WHITE HAT WITH A FEATHER ATTACHED TO IT. HE LOOKED SMART.

JAMES I AM THE HEADMASTER OF REDSCOUT. YES! I KNOW.

HE CAME A LITTLE CLOSER TO HARRY. AT THAT MOMENT A STOOL APPEARED BEHIND HIM.

SIT DOWN. JAMES SANK IN THAT WOODEN STOOL.

YESTERDAY NIGHT, YOUR FATHER CAME TO MEET ME. HE TOLD ME EVERYTHING. MINES, I KNOW EVERYTHING. JAMES LET EVERYTHING GO IN FLOW.

WE WILL SEE WHATEVER SATEN WILL DO.

YOU KNOW, YOU ARE THE 2ND MOST POWERFUL PERSON.

DON'T WORRY FOR REDSCOUT. HOW MUCH I KNOW, SATEN WILL NEVER DO ATTACKS ON ITS OWN. HE WILL OBVIOUSLY

SEND SOMEONE. AND TILL THE TIME YOU ARE HERE, THAT PERSON CAN'T DO ANYTHING. YOU WILL CRUSH HIM. SATEN WILL COME TO DO THE FINAL WORK. AND THAT IS THE THING YOU SHOULD WORRY FOR. BUT YOU KNOW ONE THING, YOUR LOCKET IS BETTER THAN SATEN'S. YOUR LOCKET SHOWS THE BROKEL WHICH YOU NEED AT THAT TIME ON THE TOP LIST. SO, YOU CAN TAKE THE ADVANTAGE OF IT.

THAT'S THE MAIN REASON WHY SATEN WANTS IT. AND YOU HAVE YOUR SUIT WHICH IS GIVEN BY JESUS CHRIST.

YOU WILL BE MUCH TENSED BECAUSE YOUR EXAMS ARE TOMORROW. BUT YOU HAVE TO NOT WORRY. YOU HAVE THE MARVELLE LOCKET.

HENRY, IT IS NOT THE EXAMS. IT IS AN EXAM IN WHICH WE WILL SORT PEOPLE FOR A GAME. WHICH TYPE OF GAME, SIR? SEE HENRY, THE MOST POWERFUL STUDENT IN THE SCHOOL IS CHOOSING. THAT STUDENT GOES IN OTHER REDSCOUT TO FIGHT WITH THE MOST POWERFUL STUDENT OF THE SCHOOL. WHOSO EVER WINS GETS A CUP.

WE ARE LOSING FROM 3 YEARS, BUT NOW WE WILL WIN. THIS TIME WE WILL SELECT YOU AND THE OTHER MOST POWERFUL STUDENT.

FOR FORMALITY YOU GIVE THE EXAM.

OK, NOW YOU CAN GO.

THANKS, FOR THE INSTRUCTIONS, HEADMASTER.

OH! THAT WAS MY RESPONSIBILITY.

JAMES WENT TO HIS ROOM AND STARTED PRACTICING.

WHOLE DAY, HE PRACTICED. JAMES MET NEITHER HALEN NOR ROELD.

AT LATE NIGHT HE SLEPT, WITH 24 BROKELS IN HIS MIND.

THE NEXT MORNING JAMES WOKE UP. IT WAS THE EXAM DAY.

JAMES GOT READY AND TOOK HIS CORD. ROELD AND HALEN JOINED HIM.

THEY ALL GOT READY AND WENT TO THE CLASSROOM.

WHEN THEY WERE ON THEIR WAY, SOMEONE JUMPED IN FRONT OF THEM.

ROELD CAME IN FRONT.

GET OUT FROM HERE, CHRISTINO. IF I WON'T.

I WILL KILL YOU. CHRISTINO TOOK OUT HIS CORD AND POINTED IT TOWARDS ROELD.

HE SHOUTED, DUNNO'. A RED LINE CAME FROM HIS CORD AND HIT ROELD.

ROELD FLEW INTO THE AIR AND WENT BACK 13 FEET BACK. ROELD GOT UP AND SAID MACKFROE!

CHRISTINO WAVED HIS CORD AND THE BROKEL WENT IN DIFFERENT DIRECTION. ROELD SAID ANOTHER BROKEL.

CHRISTINO WENT BACK AND BANGED WITH THE WALL.

ROELD WAS STANDING PROUDLY.

BUT CHRISTINO WAS IN BIG ANGER. HE GOT UP AND POINTED HIS CORD TOWARDS THE SKY. A BLUE LIGHT CAME OUT FROM THE SKY.

JAMES GOT TO KNOW THAT IT WAS A DANGEROUS BROKEL.

HE RAN TOWARDS ROELD. HE CAME IN FRONT OF HIM AND SAID PROTO. THE BROKEL STOPPED.

IT EVEN DIDN'T TOUCH HENRY. AFTER 2 SECONDS THE BROKEL STOPPED AND

HENRY'S PROTECTION WENT BACK IN HIS CORD.

CHRISTINO POINTED HIS CORD TOWARDS JAMES AND HE SAID A BROKEL.

AT THAT MOMENT, JAMES ALSO SAID A BROKEL.

IN A SECOND HENRY'S BROKEL HAD HIT CHRISTINO AND HE WAS LYING FAR ENOUGH TO SEE.

JAMES WENT TOWARDS HIM.

HE BENDS A BIT AND SAID SOMETHING.

NOW NEVER TRY TO FIGHT WITH ME. IS THAT CLEAR?

JAMES STARTED GOING FROM THERE. CHRISTINO SHOUTED, 'I WILL NOT LEAVE YOU HENRY. I WILL KILL YOU IN THE EXAM.' JAMES WENT FROM THERE, IGNORING HIM.

AFTER A MINUTE THEY CAME IN A GIGANTIC GROUND.

THERE WERE THOUSANDS OF CIRCULAR ROOMS FOR THE SELECTION OF PLAYERS.

JAMES SAID GOOD LUCK TO EVERYONE AND WENT IN HIS ROOM.

CHRISTINO WAS NOT THERE. JAMES STOOD AT HIS PLACE AND STARTED

EXAMINE THE ROOM. IT WAS A HUGE PLACE WITH NOTHING IN IT.

THERE WERE JUST TWO BIG CIRCLES PUT ON THE WALL.

ONE TELLS US THAT A STUDENT IS HOW MUCH POWERFUL THEN THE OPPONENT IN%. AND THE OTHER CIRCLE TELLS US THAT WHAT IS THE RANK IN THE WHOLE CLASS OF THE PERSON WHO IS WINNING BY HIS OPPONENT. JAMES SAID A BROKEL IN HIS MIND AND STARTED PUTTING HIS CORD IN HIS BODY. IT WAS A BROKEL FROM WHICH A PERSON'S HAND CAN ACT LIKE CORD.

AFTER A MINUTE OR TWO, CHRISTINO CAME.

HE WAS LOOKING VERY ANGRY. HE STOOD AT HIS PLACE WITHOUT SAYING A WORD.

AT THAT MOMENT A LOUDSPEAKER APPEARED IN THE CORNER OF THE ROOM.

MADAM JESSICA'S VOICE CAME FROM IT.

EVERYONE WILL START WHEN I WILL SAY. 3, 2, 1, START THE MATCH.

CHRISTINO POINTED HIS CORD TOWARDS HENRY. HE SHOUTED, 'NEONTA.' A GREEN LIGHT CAME OUT AND IT HIT HENRY.

JAMES FELL ON THE FLOOR. CHRISTINO DID AGAIN A BROKEL. JAMES WENT BACK LYING ON THE FLOOR.

CHRISTINO DID THIS BROKEL FOR 5 TIMES.

THE METER WAS SHOWING THAT CHRISTINO IS POWERFUL THEN JAMES BY 60%.

THERE WAS STILL NO RANK WRITTEN ON THE SECOND METER.

CHRISTINO SEIZED JAMES AND MADE HIM FALL WITH A THUD. HE DID LIKE THIS FOR 2 TIMES. THE THIRD TIME HE THREW HIM VERY FAR. EVERYWHERE SMOKE WAS BECAUSE THE WALL HAS BROKEN. BUT AS JAMES GOT UP, THE PIECES OF THE WALL AGAIN JOINED AND MADE THE WALL.

JAMES GOT UP. HE PUT HIS HAND IN THE FRONT AND SAID A BROKEL.

THICK, BLUE LIGHT CAME FROM HIS HANDS. FROM ITS LIGHT, CHRISTINO WAS NOT SEEN.

WHEN THE LIGHT HAD FINISHED, JAMES SAW THAT CHRISTINO WAS 10 FEET UNDER THE GROUND.

BLOOD WAS COMING OUT CHRISTINO'S FOREHEAD. HIS CLOTHES WERE FILLED WITH DUST.

HIS FACE LOOKED BROWN BECAUSE A THICK LAYER OF DUST HAS COVERED HIS FACE.

THERE WERE WOUNDS AND SCRATCHES EVERYWHERE IN HIS BODY.

HE MANAGED TO COME OUT.

AS HE CAME OUT, THE GROUND AGAIN BECAME LIKE IT WAS.

JAMES MADE A FIREBALL AND THREW AT CHRISTINO. AS IT TOUCHED IT, HIS BODY TURNED INTO FIRE.

AFTER A MINUTE HE AGAIN BECAME NORMAL BUT HE WAS BADLY INJURED.

JAMES SAID A BROKEL AND BUBBLES STARTED COMING OUT FROM HIS HAND.

IF THOSE BUBBLES TOUCHÉ A PERSON, THAT PERSON GETS SO MUCH PAIN LIKE THE WHOLE EARTH HAS FALLEN ON HIM.

10 TO 12 BUBBLES HAD HIT HIM. CHRISTINO WAS SHOUTING AND WAILING WITH PAIN.

WHEN THE BUBBLES STOPPED, CHRISTINO FELL ON THE FLOOR.

HENRY'S CORD CAME OUT FROM HIS CHEST. HE PICKED IT UP AND POINTED IT TOWARDS CHRISTINO.

HE SAID A BROKEL AND ELECTRICITY CAME OUT FROM HIS CORD.

IT WAS REAL ELECTRICITY BUT IT NEVER KILLS A PERSON. IT ONLY GIVES THEM PAIN.

CHRISTINO WAS AGAIN SHOUTING WITH PAIN.

THE METER SHOWED THAT JAMES WAS 100% POWERFUL THEN CHRISTINO.

THE OTHER METER SHOWED THAT HE WAS 1ST IN THE WHOLE CLASS.

AFTER A MINUTE, FLOWERS FELLED FROM THE ROOF.

A NOTE CAME DOWN.

CONGRATULATION! JAMES COOK YOU HAVE WON BY CHRISTINO AND HE IS THE MOST POWERFUL IN THE CLASS.

HE IS THE FIRST PERSON IN THE WHOLE SCHOOL TO WIN. EVERYONE ELSE IS FIGHTING.

HE IS EVEN SELECTED IN THE LIST OF TOP 10 WINNERS. ONE TIME AGAIN CONGRATULATION!

JAMES CAME OUT OF HIS ROOM AND SAW THAT NONE WAS THERE. HE WAS ALONE IN THE LIGHT OF THE SUN.

JAMES WENT BACK TO HIS ROOM. AFTER AN HOUR HE CAME OUT AND WENT BACK TO THE GROUND.

HE STAYED THERE FOR A MINUTE AND THEN THE GATE THE OPENED. TWO PEOPLE ON A BED WERE COMING OUT.

FOUR PEOPLE WERE HOLDING THEM.

THEY WERE BADLY INJURED AND WERE GOING TO THE HOSPITAL.

AFTER A MINUTE EVERY DOOR STARTED OPENING. PEOPLE WERE COMING OUT ON THE BED.

IT WAS A BIG RUSH. JAMES WAS RUNNING HERE AND THERE TO FIND ROELD

AND HALEN. THOUSANDS OF THEM WERE
GOING OUT.

FROM A VERY FAR DISTANCE, JAMES
SAW ROELD'S HAND.

HE RAN TO HIM.

HE PUSHED EVERY ONE AND FINALLY
CAME TO HIS BED.

ROELD WAS HAVING WOUNDS
EVERYWHERE. BLOOD WAS COMING OUT
FROM HIS HEAD AND HANDS.

WHAT HAS HAPPENED TO HIM?

THE MAN WHO WAS TAKING HIM,
ANSWERED IN A GREAT HURRY.

HE HAS LOST. EVEN HIS PARTNER IS
GREATLY INJURED AND HAD LOST. THE
MATCH WAS TIE. WE ARE TAKING HIM TO
THE HOSPITAL.

THEY PICKED ROELD AND STARTED
MOVING.

HENRY'S EYES WERE FILLED WITH
TEARS.

HE WAS NOW FINDING HALEN.

A MINUTE HAD NOT PASSED WHEN
HALEN'S BED PASSED THROUGH HIM.

HE LOOKED BACK AND RECOGNIZED
THAT SHE WAS HALEN. 4 PEOPLE WERE

AROUND HER. THEY WERE SAYING THAT SHE IS 60% DEAD.

JAMES FELL ON HIS KNEES AND STARTED CRYING. JUST THEN A BOY CAME.

HE PUT HIS HAND ON HENRY'S SHOULDER.

JAMES EVERY YEAR IT HAPPENS. JAMES GOT UP AND LOOKED TOWARDS HIM.

HENRY'S BRAIN WAS CONTINUOUSLY SAYING THAT HE HAS MET HIM BEFORE.

JAMES JUST 500 PEOPLE OUT OF 60000 IS NOT IN HOSPITAL.

MOSTLY EVERYONE IS INJURED SO THEIR MATCH IS TIE.

BUT WE BOTH HAVE WON.

THERE ARE 60 HOSPITALS IN REDSCOUT WITH 70000 BEDS.

IT IS FOR EVERYONE.

THEY WILL BE ALL RIGHT AFTER A MONTH.

HIS WORDS GAVE SYMPATHY TO HENRY.

AS HE WAS GOING TO ASK HIM THAT HE HAS EVER SEEN HIM, 8 PEOPLE FROM BACK CAME.

C'MON HENRY, WE ARE THE WINNERS, WE HAVE TO CLICK PHOTOS.

ALL THE 8 PEOPLE STOOD THERE WITH THEIR HANDS FOLDED AND THEN SOMEONE CLICKED THE PHOTO.

JAMES WENT BACK TO HIS ROOM GLOOMILY.

HE WAS VERY SAD.

HE ATTENDED HIS CLASSES EVERY DAY. A MONTH HAD ALREADY PASSED BUT IT SEEMED JAMES THAT A YEAR HAS PASSED.

JAMES WENT TO THE CLASS OF SIR OCKWILL BUT HE FOUND OUT THAT IT WAS CLOSED.

SOMETHING JUST CLICKED IN HENRY'S MIND.

I HAVE JUST FORGOTTEN THAT A MONTH HAD PASSED AND NOW HE CAN GET HIS FRIENDS BACK.

HE LEAP INTO THE AIR AND WALKED TO THE GREAT HALL.

THERE WAS A LOUD NOISE OF MURMURS. HE TOOK HIS SEAT AND WAITED FOR ROELD AND HALENA.

AN HOUR HAD PASSED AND ROELD AND HALENA DIDN'T COME.

JUST AT THAT MOMENT, STUDENTS STARTED COMING FROM THE PASSAGEWAY.

EVERYONE CAME OUT OF THEIR SEATS AND WENT TO HUG THEIR FRIENDS.

JAMES ATLAS FOUND THEM. HE HUGGED THEM. NICE TO SEE YOU.

YES, WE WERE ALSO COUNTING DAYS TO SEE YOU.

THEY SAT IN THEIR CHAIR AND STARTED HAVING FOOD.

THEY ENJOYED THEIR FOOD. AFTER THE FOOD WAS FINISHED, SIR DAIFOI CAME.

HE COUGHED A BIT TO TAKE ATTENTION.

SO WE HAVE SELECTED OUR TOP 10 WINNERS, AND NOW WE ARE GOING TO RESELECT SOME OF THEM, SO ALL THE WINNERS COME ON THE STAGE.

JAMES AND OTHER 9 WINNERS WENT.

PLEASE GIVE THEM A ROUND OF APPLAUSE.

SIR DAIFOI TOOK TWO BADGES AND SHOWED THEM TO THE STUDENT.

ONE WAS OF SILVER COLOR AND THE OTHER WAS OF GOLDEN.

THE SILVER BADGE WAS NORMAL WITH SOME THINGS WRITTEN ON IT.

THE GOLD ONE WAS HAVING DIAMONDS AROUND IT. EVERYTHING WAS WRITTEN IN 3D LETTERS.

IF I PUT A SILVER BADGE ON YOU THEN THINK THAT YOU ARE NOT GOING FURTHER, IT IS JUST FOR COMING IN TOP 10. IF I PUT THE GOLD ONE THEN YOU ARE GOING FURTHER.

THERE WILL BE A SLIGHT CHANGE. 3 PEOPLE WILL BE SELECTED INSTEAD OF 2.

HE MOVED TOWARDS EVERY WINNER.

HE TOOK ANOTHER ROUND AND STARTED PUTTING BADGES.

THE FIRST 4 GOT THE SILVER BADGE. WHEN HE WENT TO THE STUDENT, (JAMES THINKS THAT HE HAS EVER SEEN HIM) HE GAVE HIM THE GOLD BADGE.

EVERYONE STARTED CLAPPING I THEIR WHOLE MIGHT.

RONALD IS SELECTED AS ONE OF THE REPRESENTATIVE FROM OUR REDSCOUT.

HE WENT TO HENRY. HE GAVE HIM THE GOLD BADGE.

EVERYONE AGAIN STARTED CLAPPING.

JAMES IS OUR SECOND REPRESENTATIVE.

HE THEN KEPT ON GIVING THE SILVER BADGES.

HE ATLAS CAME TO THE LAST BOY. HE GAVE HIM THE GOLDEN BADGE.

THEY WENT BACK TO THEIR PLACES.

THE COMPETITION WILL BEGIN AFTER A MONTH.

THERE WILL BE 3 LEVERS.

IN THE FIRST LEVER, THERE WILL BE MANY DRAGONS AND YOU HAVE TO KILL THEM. AFTER KILLING IT, THERE WILL BE A SMALL GIRL SO YOU HAVE TO TAKE HER, TO HER PARENTS.

IN THE NEXT LEER, YOU WILL BE IN A ROOM AND YOU HAVE TO COME OUT.

IN THE FINAL LEVER, YOU HAVE TO FIGHT WITH WINNER OF THE OTHER REDSCOUT.

THIS TIME THE WINNERS OF OTHER REDSCOUT WILL COME IN OUR SCHOOL. THANK YOU! YOU CAN GO BACK AND SLEEP.

JAMES WAS ATTENDING HIS CLASSES AND EVEN PREPARING FOR HIS COMPETITION. 28 HAD PASSED AND NOTHING ODD WAS THERE.

JAMES THOUGHT THAT SATEN HAS GONE SILENT.

JUST 2 DAYS WERE LEFT FOR THE COMPETITION.

AND FINALLY THE DAY HAD COME.

JAMES GOT READY IN THE CHANGING ROOM.

ROELD AND HALEN CAME IN TO MEET HIM. GOOD LUCK HENRY. I KNOW THAT YOU WILL WIN.

THANKS ROELD.

ALL THREE CAME OUT OF THE ROOM. THERE WERE LACKS OF PEOPLE SHOUTING. MANY WERE CHEERING.

SOME HAD EVEN WRITTEN HENRY'S NAME.

THERE WAS A 100INCH TV WHICH SHOWED THAT WHAT WAS HAPPENING.

IN THE GROUND, THERE WERE 6 100 FEET LONG ROOMS.

JAMES HAS TO GO IN THOSE ROOMS.

THE ROOM WAS VACANT. IT JUST HAD A SMALL CHILD TIED UP AND SOME MINIATURE DRAGONS.

I HAVE TO FIGHT WITH THEM. THEY ARE SMALL. IN A SECOND THEY WILL DIE.

JAMES WAS LOOKING VERY CONFIDENT.

JAMES WAS LAUGHING, BUT THEN THOSE SMALL DRAGONS TURNED INTO GIGANTIC RED DRAGONS. THEY WERE VERY BIG AND WERE LOOKING REAL DANGEROUS.

HENRY'S HEART WAS POUNDING WITH FEAR.

THE DRAGONS HAD CIRCLED HIM.

FIRE CAME OUT FROM THEIR MOUTH. JAMES POINTED HIS CORD IN THE SKY. HE SAID A BROKEL AND A JET OF WATER CAME. SO THE FIRE EVEN DIDN'T TOUCH HENRY.

JAMES RAN TO SAVE HIS LIFE.

THE DRAGONS WERE CONTINUOUSLY TAKING OUT FIRE FROM THEIR MOUTH.

A DRAGON BEAT JAMES FROM HIS TAIL. HE WENT FLYING AND FELL ON THE GROUND.

ANOTHER DRAGON WAS COMING TO KILL HIM.

HE GOT UP AND POINTED HIS CORD TOWARDS THE UGLY DRAGON. EXPERSO! THOUSANDS OF STONES STARTED COMING OUT FROM HENRY'S CORD BUT NOTHING MUCH HAPPED TO THE DRAGON.

NO BROKEL WAS WORKING ON THE DRAGON.

JAMES WAS JUST RUNNING HERE AND THERE, MAKING A TRY TO KILL THE DRAGON.

JAMES NEEDED TIME TO THINK BUT THE DRAGON WAS NOT GIVING HIM.

ALL THE DRAGONS ROSE INTO THE AIR. THEY POINTED THEIR CLAWS TOWARDS JAMES AND STARTED FALLING ON HIM, IN A GREAT SPEED.

JAMES KNEW THAT IF HE DON'T DO ANYTHING, HE WILL BE DEAD.

HE SAT ON THE FLOOR AND SAID A BROKEL.

AN INVISIBLE PROTECTION CAME AROUND HENRY.

THE DRAGONS BANGED WITH IT.

THEY FELL ON THE GROUND. BUT THEY DIDN'T SAY THAT THEY LOST.

THEY STARTED BANGING THEIR CLAWS WITH THE PROTECTION.

MEANWHILE JAMES WAS THINKING FOR A PLAN.

HE STOOD THERE FOR 10 MINUTES. THE PROTECTION WAS BREAKING.

JAMES FLEW INTO THE AIR AND WENT INTO THE SKY.

HE MADE A BIG HOLE IN THE ROOM.

JAMES DID A SOMERSAULT AND STARTED FALLING BACK.

HE MADE AGAIN A VERY BIG HOLE IN THE ROOM AND FELL N THE GROUND.

THERE WAS A BIG NOISE LIKE A HOUSE HAD FALLEN.

ON THE GROUND, A VERY BIG HOLE WAS MADE.

IT WAS SO BIG THAT IT CAN TAKE ALL THE DRAGONS.

JAMES CAME OUT OF THE HOLE.

HE SAID A BROKEL IN HIS MIND.

IT WAS A BROKEL FROM WHICH A PERSON'S POWER IS 1000TIMES MULTIPLIED BY HIS REAL POWER.

JAMES STARTED PUNCHING ALL THE DRAGONS.

HE PUNCHED AND KICKED THEM LIKE A PROFESSIONAL.

ALL THE DRAGONS FLEW INTO THE AIR.

JAMES ALSO FLEW INTO THE AIR AND PUNCHED THEM IN THE AIR.

THEY WENT DIRECTLY IN THE HOLE.

JAMES POINTED HIS CORD TOWARDS THE HOLE AND IT CLOSED.

THEY WERE TRYING TO COME OUT, BUT THEY CAN'T.

JAMES WAS LOOKING HAPPY.

JAMES SAW IN FRONT. A BIG DRAGON WAS STILL THERE.

HE SAID A BROKEL AND A CORD APPEARED IN HIS HANDS.

HE TOOK THE SWORD AND WENT TOWARDS HIM.

HE STABLED IT IN HIS STOMACH.

THE DRAGON WAS DEAD. HE FELL ON THE FLOOR. BUT IT WAS TOO LATE. THE DRAGON HAD STABLED HIS CLAWS ON HENRY'S HAND. BLOOD WAS SPLUTTERING OUT FROM HIS BODY.

HE PUT HIS HAND ON HIS CORD AND STARTED GOING TOWARDS THE GIRL.

THE GIRL WAS A SMALL CHILD.

SHE WAS HAVING SMALL AND BROWN HAIR.

SHE WAS WEARING A PINK DRESS. HE TRIED TO FREE HER BUT HE CAN'T.

THE ROPE WAS NOT OPENING.

EVEN FROM THE SWORD. WHEN HE WAS TRYING TO OPEN IT, A DROP OF BLOOD FELL ON IT.

THE ROPE GOT BURNED AND THE GIRL WAS FREE. JAMES WENT OUT WITH THE GIRL.

EVERYONE WAS CLAPPING AND CHEERING.

JAMES WAS DIRECTLY TAKEN TO THE HOSPITAL.

1 PERSON FROM THE OTHER REDSCOUT HAD LOST THE MATCH.

HE SAID THAT HE HAD LOST, SO THE GAME WAS OVER.

THE NEXT TASK WAS AFTER A WEEK.

JAMES WAS RESTING IN THE HOSPITAL. ROELD AND HALEN USE TO COME EVERY DAY TO MEET HIM.

THE DAY OF THE SECOND TASK CAME.

THE CLIMATE WAS SAME LIKE FIRST IT WAS.

JAMES HAS TO AGAIN FIGHT IN A ROOM.

HE WENT INSIDE IT. THERE WAS A DOOR FROM WHICH HE HAS TO COME OUT.

HE WENT TOWARDS IT. BUT SOMETHING FELL. 100S OF ZOMBIES WERE AROUND HENRY.

THERE WERE COMING TO KILL HIM. JAMES USED HIS CORD. HE SAID MANY BROKEL BUT NOTHING WAS HAPPENING TO THEM.

THEY WERE COMING MORE NEAR TO HENRY.

SWEAT WAS COMING OUT FROM HIS FOREHEAD.

HE WAS SPEECH LESS.

HE WAS NOT SURE WHAT HE WAS GOING TO SAY.

HE WAS JUST SAYING THE BROKEL WHICH WERE COMING IN HIS MIND.

HE SAID A BROKEL AND A CIRCLE OF FIRE CAME AROUND HENRY.

NO ONE WILL TRY TO COME. OR I WILL PUT THIS FIRE IN YOU.

THE ZOMBIES WERE SCARED TO COME IN FRONT.

JAMES KEPT ON DOING BROKELS.

JAMES WAS VERY SCARED.

ALL THE BEST BROKELS WERE NOT WORKING.

JAMES GOT TO KNOW WHY THESE WERE NOT WORKING.

IT WAS BECAUSE THEY WERE NOT ZOMBIES. THEY WERE GHOSTS.

A GHOST CAME IN FRONT AND HE CROSSED THE FIRE.

THE ENTIRE GHOSTS WERE NOW COMING TO KILL HENRY.

ONE GHOST CAME AND E PUT HIS MOUTH IN THE MOUTH OF HENRY. HE WAS ACTUALLY BITING HIM.

THE PAIN WAS LIKE A HOUSE HAD FALLEN ON HIM.

JAMES WENT UNCONSCIOUS. HE WAS LYING ON THE FLOOR.

HE AGAIN GOT CONSCIOUS AFTER A HOUR WHEN A PERSON HAD DONE A BROKEL ON HIM.

THAT PERSON WAS HAVING BALD HEAD, THICK EYEBROWS; HE HAD LONG HEIGHT AND WAS WEARING A BLACK HOOD. WHO ARE YOU?

A PERSON SENT BY SATEN. GIVE ME THE MARVELLE LOCKET.

I WON'T GIVE YOU. YOU HAVE TO. WHAT YOU WILL DO, IF I DON'T GIVE YOU.

REDSCOUT WOULD BE FINISHED. EVERY STUDENT WILL BE DEAD.

IF YOU GIVE US THEN THIS WAR WOULD NOT BE THERE. I WILL NEVER GIVE YOU. SO YOU ARE NOT GOING TO GIVE ME LIKE THIS.

HE TOOK OUT HIS CORD AND POINTED IT TOWARDS JAMES COOK. YOU WILL BE DEAD, ALBUS.

I AM NOT AFRAID OF DEATH. BUT YOU SHOULD BE AFRAID.

JAMES PICKED UP HIS CORD BUT IT WAS BROKEN. WHAT'S YOUR NAME? MY NAME IS GENDESK ROIT.

HE TOOK OUT HIS CORD AND STARTED DOING BROKELS. JAMES WENT BACK AND BANGED WITH A WALL.

AS HE GOT UP, HE DID ANOTHER BROKEL. JAMES FLEW INTO THE AIR AND FELL ON THE LAND WITH A THUD.

JAMES PRESSED HIS WATCH. THIS TIME HE AGAIN GOT A NEW SUIT. HE WAS AGAIN ADULT.

HE WENT TOWARDS GENDESK. HE HELD HIS HAND AND PUNCHED ON HIS STOMACH.

JAMES TOOK HIS CORD AND THREW IT. HE BENDS GENDESK'S BODY AND STARTED PUNCHING ON HIS FACE.

GENDESK HELD HENRY'S HAND AND THREW HIM AWAY.

JAMES FELL NEAR GENDESK'S CORD. HE PICKED IT UP AND AS HE WAS GOING TO DO ANY BROKEL, GENDESK FELL ON HIM.

HE STARTED PUNCHING ON HENRY'S FACE.

HE GRABBED HIS CORD AND LEFT HIM. JAMES WENT NEAR HIM AND OVERLAPPED HIS LEG. HE FELL ON THE FLOOR. JAMES SAT ON HIM AND STARTED BEATING HIM. GENDESK HELD HENRY'S FACE AND MADE HIM FALL.

HE CLIMBED ON JAMES AND STARTED BEATING HIM. THEY BOTH WERE FIGHTING WITH EACH OTHER. PEOPLE WERE NOT ABLE TO SEE IT BECAUSE HE HAS BROKEN THE CAMERA.

GENDESK HELD HENRY'S HAND AND MADE HIM PRESS IT ON HIS WATCH.

JAMES AGAIN TURNED INTO A BOY. AS JAMES WAS GOING TO PRESS IT AGAIN, THERE WAS A BANG!

GENDESK DID A BROKEL FROM WHICH HIS WATCH TURNED INTO ASHES.

JAMES WAS VERY ANGRY. GENDESK TOOK OUT HIS CORD AND DID A BROKEL

FROM WHICH JAMES WAS BADLY INJURED. HE WENT TOWARDS HIM.

REDSCOUT IS GOING TO BE DESTROYED. GENDESK SAID SOMETHING AND A SWORD APPEARED IN HIS HANDS.

HE GAVE IT TO HENRY. USE THIS TO KILL THE GHOSTS.

WHY ARE YOU HELPING ME? BECAUSE IF YOU DON'T WIN THIS COMPETITION, OUR WORK WILL NOT BE DONE.

JAMES GOT UP. THE GHOSTS WERE BACK. HE KILLED THEM WITH HIS SWORD.

HE OPENED THE GATE AND CAME OUT.

ONE STUDENT FROM THEIR REDSCOUT HAD LOST.

THE FINAL MATCH WAS AFTER A WEEK AND JAMES WAS AGAIN IN THE HOSPITAL.

HE WAS UNABLE TO TELL ANYONE THAT WHAT HAS HAPPENED WITH HIM.

THE NEXT DAY HE WAS IN A GIGANTIC GROUND. THERE WERT NOW NO ROOMS BUT THERE WERE THOUSANDS OF ROCKS.

PEOPLE WERE CHEERING AND SOME WERE TALKING AND LAUGHING.

THE RULE WAS THAT, IF ANYONE IS 90% DEAD, THEN THE OPPONENT WILL WIN.

TWO MATCHES WERE TAKING PLACE.

JAMES COOK VS. JACKIE SHAROF

RONALD JUCKENBERG VS. EMILIE DASOSA

RONAL AND EMILIE WAS IN OTHER GROUND.

JACKIE WAS A BIG BOY. HE WAS HAVING BROWN HAIR AND RED FACE. HE WAS WEARING A BROWN COAT WITH BLACK PANT.

THE BOTH STOOD IN THEIR PLACE. THEY SHOOK HANDS AND THE MATCH STARTED.

JACKIE SAID A BROKEL. JAMES WAVED HIS CORD AND THE BROKEL WENT IN OTHER DIRECTION.

JAMES ROSE INTO THE AIR AND HE WAVED HIS CORD.

A BLUE STRIKE CAME OUT. IT HIT JACKIE. JACKIE FLEW INTO THE AIR.

JAMES ALSO FLEW AND HE KICKED HIM ON HIS CHEST.

JACKIE WAS HURT VERY MUCH. JAMES POINTED HIS CORD TOWARDS HIM AND SAID A BROKEL.

A BIG PUNCH CAME OUT FROM HIS CORD.

IT HIT JACKIE'S FACE. THE NEXT SECOND, HE WAS LYING ON THE FLOOR.

JACKIE GOT UP AND SAID A BROKEL. A GREEN LIGHT CAME OUT AND IT DIRECTLY HIT HENRY'S CORD'S TIP.

HIS CORD BUSTED. JAMES TRIED TO DO SOME BROKELS BUT HIS CORD WAS NOT WORKING.

JAMES QUICKLY PUT HIS CORD IN HIS CHEST AND STARTED CLIMBING THE WALLS.

JACKIE WAS DOING BROKELS. WHENEVER JACKIE USES TO SAY A BROKEL, HE USES TO GO FROM THAT WALL.

JACKIE WAS LOOKING IN FRONT AND JAMES WAS BACK.

JACKIE TURNED BACK AND SAID A BROKEL.

JAMES FELL ON THE LAND.

HE WENT TOWARDS HIM. HE WAVED HIS CORD. JAMES WAS NOW ATTACHED WITH A WALL. HIS BOTH THE HANDS AND LEGS WERE HANDCUFFED.

JACKIE WAS HAVING A KNIFE AND WAS COMING TO STABLE IT.

WHEN HE WAS VERY NEAR, JAMES SAID A BROKEL.

A BLUE LIGHT CAME OUT FROM HIS BODY.

EVERYWHERE WAS JUST SMOKE. WHEN THE SMOKE HAS GONE, PEOPLE SAW THAT JACKIE WAS LYING ON THE FLOOR.

JAMES WAS FREE WITH HIS HANDCUFFS.

JAMES WAS NOT ABLE TO DO ANY OTHER BROKELS NOW.

HIS CORD WAS BADLY DAMAGED.

JACKIE GOT UP AND SAID A BROKEL. RED LIGHT CAME OUT AND HIT HENRY.

JAMES WAS CRYING AND WAILING WITH PAIN.

THE BROKEL STOPPED. JAMES WAS SITTING ON HIS KNEES.

SUDDENLY, A LONG LINE OF CRATES CAME. JAMES ROSE INTO THE AIR AND

STARTED BANGING WITH THEM. BLOOD WAS COMING OUT FROM HIS BODY.

THE NEXT SECOND, HE WAS BANGING WITH THE STONES.

JACKIE PICKED UP A STONE AND STARTED MOVING TOWARDS HIM.

HE THREW THE CORD AND WAS JUST GOING T FALL IT WHEN SOMETHING HAPPENED.

JAMES PICKED UP HIS CORD AND SAID A BROKEL FROM WHICH A PERSON TURNS INTO A STONE.

A VOICE CAME FROM THE FRONT.

JAMES COOK HAS WON THE COMPETITION.

JAMES FELL ON HIS KNEES AND STARTED CRYING.

FROM THE OTHER GROUND, RONALD CAME.

THEY BOTH WERE GIVEN A BEAUTIFUL CUP.

THERE WAS A BIG FEAST. WHILE HE WAS HAVING HIS FEAST, JAMES REMEMBERED SOMETHING.

HE THOUGHT TO ASK RONAL THAT HAVE HE SEEN HIM.

HE STARTED GOING TOWARDS RONALD.

HI! I WANT TO ASK YOU SOMETHING. WHAT YOU WANT TO ASK HENRY?

HAVE I SEEN YOU BEFORE?

JAMES YOU KNOW ME VERY WELL. I AM THAT ONLY RONALD WHO HELPED YOU ON THE EARTH.

I AM YOUR BEST FRIEND. JAMES WAS SPEECHLESS BY THESE WORDS.

SIR DAIFOI SEND ME. MINES JOHN, WATSON AND CHRIS ARE ALSO HERE.

YES, THEY ARE WITH US. RONALD POINTED HIS FINGER TOWARDS SOMEONE.

3 PEOPLE WERE STANDING THERE. JAMES GOT TO KNOW THAT THEY WERE HIS FRIENDS.

JAMES WENT AND HUGGED THEM. THEY TALKED FOR A LONG TIME.

AFTER 2 HOURS, THE FEAST WAS OVER AND EVERYONE WENT TO SLEEP.

IT WAS MID NIGHT, WHEN JAMES HEARD A NOISE.

HE CAME OUT OF HIS ROOM AND STARTED FOLLOWING THE NOISE.

THE NOISE WAS COMING LOUDER. WHEN JAMES CAME OUTSIDE SIR OCKWILL'S CLASS, HE SAW SOMEONE.

HE WAS WEARING A BLACK HOOD. HE WAS HOLDING A CHAIN.

5 TO 6 PEOPLE WERE BACK OF HIM.

WHO ARE YOU? THAT MAN TURNED TOWARDS HIM.

I AM A SPIRIT. WHY HAVE YOU COME HERE? SATEN HAS SENT ME TO GET THE FORMULA.

JUST THEN A BOY CAME OUT. HE WAS WALKING BUT HE WAS A SLEEP.

THE SPIRIT ROLLED HIS CHAIN AND THREW AT THAT BOY.

THE CHAIN OVER LAPPED THE NECK OF THE BOY.

THE SPIRIT PULLED HIM. HE THREW HIM TOWARDS THE PEOPLE WHO WERE BACK OF HIM.

A PERSON TOOK OUT A THING AND STABLED IT IN THE CHILD'S CHEST.

SMALL QUANTITY OF LIQUID CAME OUT FROM HIS BODY.

WHAT ARE YOU DOING? TAKING THE FORMULA.

AFTER SAYING THIS, THEY ALL VANISHED. THE BOY GOT UP.

HE ROARED AND STARTED KILLING HENRY.

JAMES RAN TO SAVE HIS LIFE. HE WENT IN SIR DAIFOI'S OFFICE.

SIR, THEY HAVE COME.

HE TOOK A CORD AND HID UNDER A TABLE. HEADMASTER WAS BEWILDERED.

JAMES OPENED HIS LOCKET AND STARTED LEARNING SOME BROKEL.

JAMES CAME OUT AND SAID THE BROKEL.

THE BOY FELL ON THE LAND.

SIR, SATEN IS DOING ATTACK. JAMES TOLD HIM EVERYTHING.

JAMES YOU ARE THE MOST POWERFUL PERSON IN THE REDSCOUT.

I GIVE YOU THE RESPONSIBILITY TO STOP THIS.

YOU SHOULD NOW GO BACK. AND NO ONE SHOULD GET TO KNOW A SNIFF OF IT.

JAMES DIDN'T SLEPT THIS NIGHT AT ALL.

HE WAS THINKING ABOUT THE ATTACK.

THE NEXT DAY, JAMES WAS CALLED BY SIR DAIFOI.

HE WENT TO HIS CABIN.

COME HENRY, COME. I WAS WAITING FOR YOU ONLY.

I WANT TO TELL YOU A VERY IMPORTANT THING. WHAT IMPORTANT THING?

THERE WERE 2 MORE ATTACKS. HENRY'S HEART STARTED POUNDING.

WHO WERE ATTACKED? HENRY, I AM REALLY VERY SORRY TO SAY THAT THEY WERE RONAL AND HALEN.

'WHAT THE...' SAID JAMES IN A TONE OF SHOCK.

I WANT TO MEET THEM. WHERE THEY ARE?

YOU CAN'T MEET THEM. WHY CAN'T I MEET THEM?

BECAUSE THEY ARE NOT IN REDSCOUT. HE TOOK THEM AND THE OTHER CHILD WITH THEM.

JAMES I KNOW THAT I AM SENDING YOU IN A POOL OF DEATH BUT I CAN'T DO ANYTHING.

IT IS AN ORDER FROM THE GOVERNMENT. YOU HAVE TO GO IN THE PALACE AND FIND OUT THE REASON.

TEARS ROLLED DOWN FROM HENRY'S CHEEKS. I AM GOING. JAMES STARTED GOING. HE HAD JUST GONE A FOOT AWAY WHEN SIR DAIFOI CALLED HIM.

HE PLACED A WATCH ON THE TABLE. YOU WILL NEED T. IT WAS THE WATCH WHICH WAS BROKEN IN THE COMPETITION.

JAMES TOOK IT AND WENT ON THE WAY TO THE PALACE.

THE PALACE WAS A VERY BVIG BUILDING. IT WAS AS BIG AS A SMALL VILLAGE. IT WAS OF WHITE CLOUT.

THE MAIN BUILDING WAS HAVING 2 BIG BLACK STATUE WAS THERE. IT WAS SOMETHING LIKE A DANGEROUS OWL WITH CLAWS POINTING TOWARDS HIM.

AT THE BOTTOM, THERE WAS A BIG DOOR. IT WAS OPENED. TWO PEOPLE WERE STANDING WITH CORD.

AT THE TOP, THERE WAS A GIGANTIC STATUE. IT WAS ACTUALLY SATEN. HE WENT TOWARDS THE PEOPLE.

HE WORE HIS SUIT. HE TOOK OUT HIS CORD AND SAID A BROKEL POINTING TOWARDS HIM. THE MAN FLEW IN THE AIR AND FELL BACK.

THE OTHER ONE TURNED TOWARDS HIM. JAMES MADE HIS PUNCH BLUE AND BEAT ON HIS FACE. THEY WERE LYING ON THE FLOOR.

HE WENT IN THE PALACE. NONE WAS SAYING A WORD BECAUSE THEY THOUGHT THAT HE MUST BE A PERSON WORKING FOR THEM.

JAMES WAS NOW IN THE PLACE WHERE KINGS AND OTHER PEOPLE SIT.

SATEN WAS SITTING IN THE MIDDLE. HE WAS TALKING WITH HIS ASSISTANT. SO, HOW OUR PLAN IS GOING?

THE ASSISTANT STARTED SAYING. SIR, WE HAVE GOT THE 3 STUDENT. TOMORROW WE WILL KILL HIM. AFTER THEY ARE KILLED, WE WILL GET THE THING FROM WHICH WE THE THING WILL BE MADE AND WE CAN TAKE THE FORMULAS.

A PERSON SITTING IN THE END RAISED HIS HAND. HE GOT UP AND STARTED SAYING. SIR, I HAVE A QUESTION.

WE JUST NEEDED 1 STUDENT TO GET THE THING BUT WHY 3.

SATEN SAW TOWARDS HIS ASSISTANT AND SHOOK HIS HEAD. HIS ASSISTANT GOT UP AND STARTED EXPLAINING.

WE HAVE 3 BECAUSE OF A REASON. THE GIRL AND THAT BOY ARE USELESS. THEY ARE THE FRIENDS OF HENRY.

IF THEY WILL BE DEAD, JAMES WILL BE VERY ANGRY. HE WILL COME TO KILL THE PERSON WHO IS DOING THIS.

THAT PERSON WILL BE DEAD. AS HE WILL BE DEAD, A SWORD WILL COME OUT AND DEFINITELY KILL HIM.

THAT PERSON SAT DOWN. SATEN WAS NOW LOOKING MORE PROUD. SO WHAT WE HAVE TO DO NEXT.

SATEN POINTED TOWARDS A PERSON. I WANT THE PLAN BOOK. THAT MAN WENT TO GET THE BOOK. JAMES WAS FOLLOWING HIM.

THEY CAME IN A ROOM. THAT MAN PUT HIS HAND ON THE WALL. A SHELVE CAME. OUT. IT WAS HAVING JUST ONE BOOK.

JAMES HYPNOTIZED THAT PERSON. HE FELL ON THE FLOOR. JAMES TOOK THAT BOOK AND OPENED IT.

THE CHAIN PERSON WILL GO IN REDSCOUT.

HE WILL TRAP 1 PERSON.

WE WILL SCAN HIS BLOOD.

THE SCANNED BLOOD WILL BE PUT IN AN INSTRUMENT CALLED FORMULAE COLLECTOR.

THERE WILL BE ATTACKS EVERY DAY.

THIS MUCH WAS ONLY WRITTEN IN THAT BOOK. JAMES WAS JUST THINKING ABOUT THE STUDENTS.

HE RAN TO FIND THE PLACE WHERE THEY WERE HIDDEN. HE MET A PERSON.

HEY, CAN YOU TELL ME, WHERE THE PRISONERS ARE. NO I CAN'T TELL.

JAMES TOOK OUT HIS CORD AND POINTED TOWARDS HIM. TELL ME OR I WILL KILL YOU! THAT PERSON STARTED SHIVERING WITH FEAR.

OK! OK! I WILL TELL. GO STRAIGHT THEN LEFT, RIGHT AND YOU WILL COME AT THE END OF THIS PALACE.

KNOCK THE FLOOR AND YOU WILL BE IN YOUR DESTINY. JAMES DID EXACTLY LIKE HE HAS SAID. HE KNOCKED THE FLOOR AND A DUNGEON APPEARED.

HE WENT INSIDE IT. HALEN, RONALD AND THE OTHER STUDENT WERE SITTING THERE.

THEY WERE UNCONSCIOUS. JAMES RAN TO HUG THEM. BUT SOMETHING HAPPENED. HE FELL SOMEWHERE.

IT WAS AN UNDERGROUND PLACE. NOTHING WAS THERE, LEAVING A CHAIN. IT WAS THE ONLY CHAIN WHICH THAT PERSON USED.

HE PICKED IT UP. JAMES STARTED BANGING IT WITH THE WALLS. HE WAS JUST PRACTICING WHEN SOMETHING HAPPENED.

THE FRONT WALL WAS NOW A BIG ROOM WITH A BIG DOOR. JAMES WAS AWESTRUCK. HE OPENED THE DOOR.

SOMETHING OR SOMEBODY WAS THERE IN THAT DARK LIGHT. A THING CAME OUT. IT WAS A GIGANTIC BLUE PERSON. HE WAS AS BIG AS A 3 STORY HOUSE.

HE WAS VERY FAT AND GREEN. HE WAS LOOKING VERY UGLY. HE WAS ACTUALLY MONSTER. HE WAS HOLDING SOMETHING.

IT WAS A BASEBALL BAT. HE WAVED IT AND BANGED WITH HENRY. JAMES FLEW IN THE AIR AND FELL ON THE LAND.

THAT THING THREW HIS BAT AND JUMPED ON HENRY. THAT THING SCRATCHED JAMES WITH IS LONG NAILS.

BLOOD WAS COMING OUT FROM HENRY'S FACE. THAT THING WAS CONTINUOUSLY TRYING TO KILL JAMES BUT JAMES WAS ROLLING ON THE GROUND SO EVERY TIME HE WAS SAVED.

JAMES TOOK OUT HIS CORD AND STARTED SAYING BROKEL BUT NOTHING HAPPENED.

JAMES NOTICED TOWARDS A CAMERA.

HE FOUND OUT THE REAL MATTER. THE CAMERA WAS CONTROLLING THE MONSTER.

JAMES JUMPED IN THE AIR AND SOMEHOW ATTACHED HIMSELF WITH THE CAMERA.

HE STARTED SHOOK IT. WHEREVER HE USE TO SHAKE, THAT MONSTER USE

TO GO THERE. THE MONSTER JUMPED IN THE AIR AND BANGED HIS CLAWS WITH HENRY'S FACE.

JAMES WAS NOW LAID ON THE FLOOR. HE PICKED UP HIS BAT AND BROKE THE CAMERA.

THE MONSTER HAD VANISHED. JAMES NOW WENT TOWARDS THE ROOM. IT WAS A VACANT ROOM. IT JUST HAD A PIECE OF PAPER. JAMES PICKED IT UP AND STARTED READING IT.

SATEN IS VERY NEAR. HE IS WITH YOU WHEN LIGHT FALLS. YOU CAN'T WALK ON IT BECAUSE IT IS INVISIBLE.

IT IS THE KEY FOR YOUR ROOM. OPEN IT AND YOU WILL BE IN THE PLACE WHERE THE FORMULA IS KEPT.

HE IS NOT SATEN BUT HALF SATEN. HE IS JUST THE THING FROM WHICH THE PALACE GETS TO KNOW, WHAT TO DO.

YOU CAN'T KILL HIM AND CAN'T WALK ON IT.

JAMES DIDN'T UNDER STAND ANYTHING. HE KEPT THE PAPER AND WENT BACK TO HALEN AND RONALD.

HE SCANNED THEIR BODY AND SOME RECOMMEND CAME. IT SAID THAT THEY NEED WARMTH OF REAL FIRE.

THE WARMTH SHOULD BE VERY MUCH. AN IDEA CLICKED IN HIS MIND.

HE TOOK THE ROUND THING WHICH CLOSED THE BASEMENT. HE TIED THEM WITH IT AND CLOSED THEM.

HE SAID A BROKEL FROM WHICH NO ONE CAN OPEN IT LEAVING HENRY. HE SAW TOWARDS HIS SUIT.

A BIG PIPE WAS THERE. HE TOOK IT AND SOMETHING LIKE WATER STARTED COMING OUT.

IT WAS NOT WATER BUT PETROL. HE MADE THE WHOLE PLACE WET WITH PETROL. HE WENT OUT AND SLEPT SOMEWHERE.

THE NEXT MORNING HE GOT UP. HE WENT TOWARDS THE PALACE. HE KILLED THE 2 PEOPLE.

JAMES TOOK OUT A MATCHSTICK. HE LIGHTS A FIRE AND THREW TOWARDS THE PALACE.

SOON THE FIRE CAUGHT THE WHOLE PALACE. JAMES WORE A FIRE POOF SUIT.

HE BECAME INVISIBLE AND WENT IN THE PALACE.

JAMES WENT STRAIGHT TOWARDS THE BASEMENT. WHENEVER HE USE TO SEE A PERSON USING HIS CORD, HE USE TO LIGHT A FIRE ON HIM.

AFTER 3 HOURS, EVERYONE WAS DEAD, LEAVING SATEN AND SOME PEOPLE WHICH WERE VERY NEAR TO HIM.

THEY HAD NOT COME ONLY IN THE PALACE. WHEN THE FIRE STOPPED, JAMES WENT IN THE BASEMENT.

THE THREE STUDENTS WERE LYING ON THE FLOOR. THEY WERE UNCONSCIOUS BUT CAN BE PICKED UP.

JAMES TOOK THEM TO REDSCOUT. THEY WERE IN THE HOSPITAL FOR 1 MONTH.

SATEN HAS DONE NOTHING IN ONE MONTH. FEBRUARY HAD ARRIVED AND EVERYTHING WAS NORMAL.

JAMES HAD TOLD EVERYTHING TO HALEN AND RONALD. JAMES WAS GOING TO THE TRAINING CLASS 2.

HE SAT DOWN ON HIS CHAIR. MADAM POMFREY WHO WAS THE CLASS TEACHER WAS TELLING THEM BROKEL.

POINT YOUR CORD TOWARDS THE STATUE WHICH IS IN FRONT OF YOU. EVERYONE GET UP AND SAY 'TURN IN FREDAY' THINK A LIVING ANIMAL IN YOUR MIND AND IT WILL CHANGE IN IT.

SO, EVERYONE SAY 'TURN IN FREDAY' JAMES WAS NOT DOING THESE THINGS. HE WAS JUST THINKING ABOUT THE RIDDLE.

RONALD'S STATUE TURNED INTO A GIANT CAT AND HALEN'S INTO A SPIDER.

THE STUDENTS WERE HAVING A FUN TIME. THEY USE TO MAKE LIONS AND MAKE OTHER STUDENTS AFRAID.

OK, SO OUR BROKEL TEACHER 2 IS NOT PRESENT HERE, SO I WILL TELL YOU ABOUT THIS.

MADAM POMFREY KEPT ON SAYING THOUSANDS OF YEAR'S BACK A PERSON WROTE IT. HE WAS VERY INTERESTED IN DOING BROKEL.

HE INVENTED THIS THING. HE WAS EARNING MONEY FROM IT BUT A CASE WAS REGISTERED ON HIM AND BLAA BLAA BLA......

THE CLASS WAS OVER. JAMES WANTED A REST SO HE WENT IN HIS ROOM. HE LIES ON THE BED AND FELL ASLEEP.

HE WOKE UP WITH A SOUND. I AM YOUR HEADMASTER. 10 PEOPLE HAVE ATTACKED REDSCOUT. I WANT ALL THE CHAMPIONS TO FIGHT WITH THEM AND ALL THE TEACHERS COME IN MY ROOM.

JAMES TOOK HIS CORD AND RAN TO THE PLACE WHERE THEY HAD COME. ALL THE 9 PEOPLE WERE PRESENT THERE.

THEY WERE FIGHTING WITH 10 MASKED PEOPLE. JAMES STARTED DOING BROKELS BUT NOTHING MUCH.

A PERSON MADE A U.F.O AND THREW IT TOWARDS HENRY. IT TOOK JAMES IN IT AND THEN IT BLASTED.

JAMES WAS BADLY INJURED. 2 PEOPLE WERE UNCONSCIOUS. JAMES HID IN A PLACE AND STARTED LEARNING BROKELS.

HE CAME OUT AND SAID, 'VOGLE DOGGLE.' THEIR BODY TURNED INTO JELLY AND THEN IT TURNED INTO WATER.

THE WATER ALSO GOT BURNED AND VANISHED.

JAMES TOOK THE 2 PEOPLE IN THE HOSPITAL. HE WENT TO SIR DAIFOI'S OFFICE.

COME HENRY, COME. I WAS WAITING FOR YOU ONLY. SIR, WHAT WILL HAPPEN NOW.

HENRY, 5 STUDENTS ARE MISSING. PUT YOUR WHOLE BRAIN IN THAT RIDDLE. TRY, HENRY, TRY.

OK, NOW YOU HAVE TO GO. IT'S THE TIME FOR YOUR SCIENCE CLASS.

JAMES TOOK HIS BOOKS AND WENT TO THE CLASS.

HELLO! EVERYONE. I WILL TEACH YOU TODAY SOMETHING INTERESTING.

CAN ANYONE TELL ME THAT HOW SHADOWS ARE FORMED? CAN YOU TELL ME SOLAR ECLIPSE AND LUNAR ECLIPSE? SOME FACTS ABOUT THEM. NO, OK I WILL TELL YOU.

HE PLACED A BULB, BIG WOODEN STATUE, 3 BALLS AND A TORCH.

OK FIRST I WILL TEACH YOU SHADOWS.

OPEN PAGE 97 IN YOUR BOOK. EVERY ONE OPENED IT. HE PICKED UP A TORCH AND A STATUE.

I GUESS THAT EVERYONE KNOW WHAT IS MATTER. THIS MATTER IS CALLED OPAQUE OBJECT.

LIGHT CAN NEVER PASS FROM AN OPAQUE OBJECT. WHEN LIGHT FALLS ON AN OPAQUE OBJECT THEN SHADOW IS CREATED.

HE ON THE TORCH AND PLACED IT IN THE FRONT OF THE STATUE. A SHADOW WAS CREATED.

OK, SO IS THAT CLEAR? I WILL TELL YOU AN INTRESTING FACT ABOUT SHADOW.

A PERSON CAN NEVER WALK ON HIS SHADOW. SHADOW WILL BE ALWAYS WITH YOU WHEN LIGHT FALLS.

SOMETHING HAS JUST CLICKED IN HENRY'S MIND. HE REPEATED THIS SENTENCE.

HE GOT UP AND RAN FROM THE CLASS. HALEN AND RONALD FOLLOWED HIM.

THEY CAME IN HENRY'S ROOM. WHAT HAPPENED HENRY. SHADOW IS THE KEY.

BUT HOW? IN THE PAPER WHAT WAS WRITTEN? IT SAID THAT YOU CAN'T WALK ON IT AND IT IS ALWAYS WITH YOU WHEN LIGHT FALLS.

AND SHADOW IS ALWAYS WITH YOU WHEN LIGHT FALLS. 'AND YOU CAN'T WALK ON IT,' RONALD ADDED. 'EXACTLY' SAID HENRY.

I WILL GO. YOU TWO STAY HERE AND WAIT FOR INSTRUCTIONS. BUT WHERE IS THE DOOR.

JAMES TOOK OUT HIS CORD AND SAID 'MYSCONICO.' THE SHELVES HIS ROOM STARTED SEPARATING.

A DOOR APPEARED. JAMES MADE HIS SHADOW IN SUCH A DIRECTION THAT IT MET WITH THE LOCK.

THE DOOR OPENED. JAMES WENT INSIDE IT.

It was very cold. James opened the next door. 5 tables were there.

5 students lay on it. Every table had one spirit. They were holding a knife.

Someone was standing at the corner of the room. He was Saten.

Saten turned towards him. Come Henry. I knew that you will come.

The formula is created. He pointed towards a big bottle which had blue liquid.

THAT IS THE FORMULA. YOU KNOW HENRY, YOU ARE A BIG FOOL. YOU KNOW EVERYTHING WAS FIXED.

WHEN YOU WERE ON EARTH AND HAD COME TO FIND OUT ABOUT ME, THAT WAS TOO FIXED.

I KNEW THAT THE 5 PEOPLE ARE YOU AND YOUR FRIENDS BUT IT WAS A PART OF THE PLAN.

WE SAW THAT YOU WERE WITH US IN THE PALACE. I ONLY GAVE YOU THE RIDDLE SO THAT YOU CAN COME HERE AND I CAN KILL YOU.

EVERYTHING WAS FIXED. NOW IT WILL BE YOUR LAST BREATH.

SATEN STARTED LAUGHING. JAMES TOOK OUT HIS CORD AND STARTED DOING BROKELS. THEY KEPT ON DOING DUEL FOR 5 MINUTES. SATEN ORDERED HIS IN 1 SPIRIT TO KILL THE BOY LAID ON THE TABLE.

AS HE WAS GOING TO KILL HIM, JAMES KILLED THE SPIRIT.

THEN HE KILLED ALL THE SPIRITS.

SATEN SAID A BROKEL AND JAMES ALSO. BLUE LINE CAME OUT FROM THEIR CORD AND MET WITH EACH OTHER.

HENRY'S HAIR WAS FLYING. HIS JACKET WAS TOO FLYING. JAMES LOST THAT DUEL. HE FELL ON THE GROUND.

JAMES DIDN'T KNOW WHAT HE IS GOING TO DO. HE SAID A BROKEL AND THE GOLDEN BALL ROSE INTO THE AIR.

IT BROKE THE FORMULA FILTER AND BANGED WITH SATEN. SATEN SHOUTED, KILL HIM.

7 SPIRITS CAME OUT FROM SATEN'S GOLDEN BALL. SATEN WENT IN THE GOLDEN POT AND IT VANISHED.

JAMES SAID A SPELL FROM WHICH THE 5 STUDENTS TRANSPORTED. JAMES RAN AS FAST AS HE COULD TO SAVE HIS LIFE.

HE WAS BADLY INJURED. JAMES RAN TOWARDS THE DOOR. HE OPENED IT AND CLOSED IT QUICKLY.

ALL THE 5 STUDENTS WERE THERE. THEY HAD TO NOW GO FROM THE OTHER DOOR. ALL THE SPIRITS WERE LOCKED BUT ONE HAD ESCAPED FROM THE DOOR.

JAMES SHOUTED, 'RUN, EVERYBODY RUN.' EVERYONE STARTED RUNNING. JAMES SHOUTED, 'HALEN OPEN THE GATE.' THE GATE WAS OPENED.

THEY RAN AND CLOSED THE GATE. HALEN, RONALD I WILL TELL YOU EVERYTHING BUT FIRST TAKE THEM TO THE HOSPITAL.

JAMES WENT TO SIR DAIFOI'S OFFICE. SIR, I DID IT. JAMES TOLD HIM EVERYTHING FROM STARTING TO END.

JAMES YOU HAVE DONE A NOBLE WORK AND YOU SHOULD GET A REWARD.

SIR DAIFOI TOOK A BIG MEDAL AND GAVE IT TO HENRY. JAMES GO JOIN THE FEAST.

WE WILL CELEBRATE THIS DAY. FROM TOMORROW THE SCHOOL WILL BE CLOSED.

JAMES WAS ON CLOUD NINE. HE WENT TO THE FEAST. HE ENJOYED IT.

THE NEXT DAY JAMES WAS IN HIS FATHER'S HOUSE. IT WAS THE BEST YEAR FOR HENRY.

WHEN JAMES RETURNED BY HIS HOUSE, THE HEADMASTER CALLED HIM.

HENRY, I HAVE TO SAY SOMETHING. YOU KNOW THIS IS NOT A REAL WORLD. ALL THE PEOPLE WHO ARE IN REDSCOUT INCLUDING ME ARE NOT REAL.

YOU ARE GOING BACK ON EARTH. THIS WAS JUST A TRAINING SESSION FOR YOU.

YOU ARE GOING IN SOME OTHER WORLD. SATEN WAS ALSO FAKE AND YOUR WATCH ALSO.

YOU WILL NOT REMEMBER ANYTHING WHEN YOU WILL GO ON EARTH. WE HAVE COME FROM THE CONSTITUTION.

IN 1 HOUR, WE ARE GOING TO VANISH AND NOW YOU ARE GOING ON EARTH.

WHAT ARE YOU SAYING? HE SAID AND JAMES WAS BACK AGAIN ON EARTH.

HE WAS IN A ROOM. HE SAW THAT SOMEONE STANDING THERE. A GIRL WITH CURLY HAIR WAS STANDING FACE TO FACE WITH A MAN.

HE WAS HAVING BROWN HAIR AND WAS WEARING A BLACK SUIT.

OK, I AM YAHYA ASHRAF, THE AUTHOR OF THIS BOOK. I KNOW THAT THIS BOOK IS NOT END BUT IT HAS TO BE END LIKE. I HAVE TO WRITE THE SECOND PART ALSO.

I DIDN'T HAD THE TIME TO FINISH IT. SO MY SECOND BOOK WHICH WILL BE THE SECOND PART WILL RELEASE IN AUGUST 2016 AND YOU CAN BUY IT FROM ALL ONLINE BOOKSTORES.. THE FRONT COVER OF THIS BOOK TELLS THAT WHAT WILL HAPPEN NEXT. BY.

THE END
WAIT FOR THE 2ND PART